Praise for *The Ne*

"Shacochis's assets as a writer—h[...]
for contemporary speech, his in[...]
inarticulate lives . . . Mr. Shacoch[...]
reluctant to barter their hopes."

—Michiko Kakutani,
The New York Times

"**A remarkable storyteller** . . . From such daring and craft comes prose capable of both fantastic revelation and familiar observations."

—*People*

"Shacochis seduces his readers into the alien territories he has made his own."

—*The Detroit News*

"Shacochis is an inventive storyteller, sensitive to the land and to the past. . . . He plays the full range of language."

—*The Milwaukee Journal*

"Rich and sensual, intensely imagined stories . . . by **a writer who can both enchant and teach.**"

—*Houston Chronicle*

"Shacochis is a master of voices. . . . In *The Next New World* he roams about through history and across the globe, tethering his wit to a sense of . . . political conscience. . . . **Sometimes more is more.**"

—*The Miami Herald*

"Shacochis's writing shines."

—*The Baltimore Sun*

"There is an up-to-the-minute wildness about this writer. . . . He has the ability to sketch a character in a line . . . and **his sentences are a marvelous, rare combination of clarity and richness.**"

—*L.A. Daily News*

CONTEMPORARY AMERICAN FICTION

THE NEXT NEW WORLD ·

Bob Shacochis won the 1985 American Book Award for his
first collection of stories, *Easy in the Islands*. Among his many
other honors and awards are the American Academy of Arts
and Letters Rome Prize, a James Michener Award, a grant
from the National Endowment for the Arts, and *Playboy*'s
Best New Fiction Award. His journalism appears frequently in
Harper's Magazine, where he is a contributing editor. He is
currently at work on a novel set in Virginia and the Caribbean.

THE
NEXT
NEW
WORLD

BOB SHACOCHIS

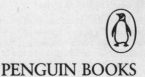

PENGUIN BOOKS

PENGUIN BOOKS
Published by the Penguin Group
Viking Penguin, a division of Penguin Books USA Inc.,
40 West 23rd Street, New York, New York 10010, U.S.A.
Penguin Books Ltd, 27 Wrights Lane, London W8 5TZ, England
Penguin Books Australia Ltd, Ringwood, Victoria, Australia
Penguin Books Canada Ltd, 2801 John Street,
Markham, Ontario, Canada L3R 1B4
Penguin Books (N.Z.) Ltd, 182–190 Wairau Road,
Auckland 10, New Zealand

Penguin Books Ltd, Registered Offices:
Harmondsworth, Middlesex, England

First published in the United States of America by
Crown Publishers, Inc., 1989
Reprinted by arrangement with Crown Publishers, Inc.
Published in Penguin Books 1990

10 9 8 7 6 5 4 3 2 1

Publisher's Note: This is a work of fiction. The characters, incidents, and dialogues are
products of the author's imagination and are not to be construed as real. Where the names
of actual persons, living or dead, are used, the situations, incidents, and dialogues con-
cerning those persons are entirely fictional and are not intended to depict any actual
events or change the entirely fictional nature of the work.

Grateful acknowledgment is given to the following magazines where stories in this
edition originally appeared:
"Stolen Kiss," copyright © 1982 by Bob Shacochis, originally appeared in *Paris Review*.
"Where Pelham Fell," copyright © 1985 by Bob Shacochis, originally appeared in
Esquire. "I Ate Her Heart," copyright © 1986 by Bob Shacochis, originally appeared in
The New Virginia Review. "Celebrations of the New World," copyright © 1985 by Bob
Shacochis, originally appeared in *Chicago Magazine*. "The Trapdoor," copyright © 1984
by Bob Shacochis, originally appeared in *Telescope*. "Hidalgos," copyright © 1988 by
Bob Shacochis, originally appeared in *Harper's*.

Author's Note: The first line of "Les Femmes Creoles" has been lovingly pinched from
the novelist Richard Hughes's 1928 classic, *A High Wind in Jamaica, or The Innocent
Voyage*.

LIBRARY OF CONGRESS CATALOGING IN PUBLICATION DATA
Shacochis, Bob.
The next new world/Bob Shacochis.
p.   cm.
ISBN 0 14 01.2105 6
I. Title.
[PS3569.H284N49   1990]
813'.54—dc20   89–39467

Printed in the United States of America
Designed by Lauren Dong

*In memory of Bob Thompson and
Linda Maltsberger; writer, wanderer; wonders.*

CONTENTS

THE
NEXT
NEW
WORLD

LES FEMMES CREOLES: A FAIRY TALE

The two old Miss Parkers lived in bed, for the Negroes had taken away all their clothes: they were nearly starved. This happened in 1923, a year before the occupation, which was meant to set everything right, ended. They lay together in an upper-story room at Derby Hill, in the ornate mahogany bed of their parents, its headboard decorated with ormolu. On the same prickly feather mattress too where they had been born, six years apart, in the estate house built by their father in another century, those days when musicians came from New Orleans to play in the ballroom on Boxing Day, the servants were rewarded with hams, and their mother wore dresses that were heavy to carry, absurdly unsuitable to the climate, and took a year or more to arrive from seamstresses in London.

Out any of the three banks of windows in the room where the sisters now reigned, the unpeaceful contours and eruptions of land daily grew more wild across the once-industrious plantation. They spent hours in a state of enraptured emptiness, watching shadows parade off the hills and stall in the destitute fields of guinea grass, muster along the horizon of mangrove to drown in the sea once filled with ships waiting to load coffee, syrup, and cotton.

Outside the south row of windows grew an immense gnip tree, laden with fruit. Birds would flock in it, over-crowding the branches, and make quite a disharmonious racket at the crack of dawn, and Mary Elizabeth—M.E., or Emmy since birth—who was afraid of birds, would throw the last of her costume jewelry to chase off grack-les that landed on the sill. Margaret Gloriana prayed for the birds to cock their iridescent heads at her sister, to have the pleasure of seeing the hoard of cheap necklaces and embarrassing rings pitched out the window. Fare-thee-well to that whore's brooch, she would cheer—to herself, of course, since she didn't want to hurt Emmy's feelings. So much wretched tin and sixpenny glass. There went that awful tiara, the tarnished pendants, the gilt-painted earrings—how they made Margaret Gloriana's hands tremble for the few real objects they had replaced, the treasures they had been forced to sell one by one to the Syrian in his vile shop, inhaling his turpentine odor.

Yesterday, or perhaps the day before—the sisters were not at all interested in counting—Mary Elizabeth had stood in one of the south windows, her wizened body visible like a stick drawing underneath her muslin night-gown, and leaned out to pick a cluster of gnips for break-fast.

"Sir, sir," Margaret Gloriana had heard her sister call-ing matter-of-factly to someone below. Emmy had seen a barefoot old black man dodging behind the base of the tree. He was wearing dress pants, a white shirt that was too big, a black necktie that was too short, and a bowler hat with crescents cut through the dusty dome to keep his head from heating up. What's more, he had been sketching a *vévé* in the dirt with his walking stick.

"Sir," Emmy said, waving. "Behind the tree. I saw you." She implored him to gather her bird ammunition and toss it back into the room.

Margaret Gloriana sprang out of bed, forgetting both her age and her nakedness. Throughout her life she had preferred to sleep with nothing on against the cool linens, and so when all was lost she was left without even a nightshirt to cover herself. "Who could you be talking to?" she wondered out loud, wrapping herself in the single sheet they shared. Everyone they knew was dead or gone away. Everyone they didn't know was unkind. She came up behind her sister, who was flapping like a scarecrow, went to the next window over, and squinted her sharp blue eyes at the figure below, who had stepped halfway out from behind the gnip tree to marvel at them.

"Who are you?" she demanded to be told, and then decided since she was speaking to a man out in the yard, it was more practical to use outside language. "What you want, jack-o, snoopin' about? Who give you permission to draw *vévé* in we dirt?"

With a jolted expression, the man below looked at the two crones, from the ethereal Mary Elizabeth to the shroud-bound Margaret Gloriana, the long white braid of her hair dangling over the sill like a hangman's rope. One spirit beckoned him forward, one scolded him like a fierce archangel—the windows of temptation and retribution. In the excitement, Margaret Gloriana forgot that she wore no clothes; she opened her hands to brace herself and the sheet slipped to the floor. The old man's eyes enlarged even with the brim of his hat, his knees had dog-shake, he took a nervous step backward to learn if this was what they were waiting for to kill him, and then he scuttered off into

3

the bush, convinced he had seen twin harpies, a very ungodly apparition.

"White people ain' need no wanga magic," Margaret Gloriana shouted as he fled. "No carabee spells." He was the first soul to come poke around since the last family of servants had disappeared one rainy midnight, hauling what remained in the house, and the first man to have a good square wake-up-Maggie-it's-Christmas-morning look at her body, such as it was, since her days of childhood. Well, she felt giddily unashamed about it, and now that she was shouting, she had the impulse to shout more, to shout something scandalously satisfying.

"Backra bubbies on sale today!"

She felt the blood rising in her mossy cheeks, fermentation in her delicate stomach. She tried again, exhilarated by the advance she had willingly made toward shandyism and disgrace. She craned out the window, her emaciated backside thrust toward Emmy, her breasts like a mauga dog's swinging in the air.

"A fart fill your sail, you Guinee rouge!" she cried out, making a bony fist, and collapsed back into the room, alarmed at how extraordinarily good it felt to raise her voice, to say something nasty and speak in the rough island dialect she had heard all her life.

"Margaret Gloriana!" Emmy, blushing and tittering, had stooped for the sheet. She spread her arms, opened like linen wings to receive her sister. They promenaded side by side back to the bed. "Where are your principles! You sound like a *filibustier!"*

"Oh, get on," Margaret said, unconcerned. She propped herself with their one pillow, pulled out her braid, set it on her chest, and began to unwind it. It was her favorite, most gratifying act, brushing the length of her pale brittle hair, blowing the broken strands off her fingertips to the floor.

LES FEMMES CREOLES

She had a desire for a glass of ginger wine, or sherry, which she had never tasted.

"I sound just like Father, that's who."

"Thank you, I don't need to be reminded," Emmy sniffed. "Still, it's very shocking to hear it from you."

"You will live your life," Margaret Gloriana sermonized, "and I will live mine."

Emmy slid down flat and wiggled her stiff toes, imagining she was a fish at the bottom of a mustard yellow lake, which was the color left in plaster patches on the walls of the room. She tried to remember her father ever saying anything nice or gallant or uplifting to anybody. He had once traded a young female servant for a sow, the price determined by matching the girl's weight against that of the pig's. Of course, the pig was worth more. She went through the ordeal of sitting back upright, weary from being at the bottom, the austere and lonely bottom, of a yellow lake.

"Do me now, Maggie dear," she said, touching the hawksbill shell of the brush which, with their enamel chamber pot and two cracked Worcester cups, was the extent of their common wealth.

"You have such pretty hair," Margaret Gloriana said, stroking her sister's silvery, ever-slackening curls.

"Oh, but it's not as pretty as yours." The two old Miss Parkers had been saying so to each other since the beginning of time.

After several hours of tying and untying two threads she had unraveled from the hem of the sheet, the younger sister, Mary Elizabeth, announced her momentous news.

"Don't be upset," she forewarned. "I have a lover."

"You do?" Margaret Gloriana, who had been staring at a blue beetle on the ceiling, sat straight up. "How can you?" Out of respect for her sister's sensitive circumstance, she looked merely doubtful, although her reaction could have been far more dramatic.

"Why, yes, I do," said Emmy, intransigent, feeling revitalized with confidence now that her secret was out in the open. "He has a gold tooth."

The present vacancy of life expanded out of focus. Margaret Gloriana folded her weightless hands and thought for a minute before she spoke again. "You have given yourself back to Christ Our Lord," she concluded, famous at Derby Hill for her uninspired good sense. "I thought you'd gotten over that ages ago. When they burned the church."

"I did," Emmy agreed. "What good is it to love someone if you can't even go to his house and have lovely conversations with his guests? I don't see the point."

Margaret Gloriana shifted restlessly, her shoulder blades scraping against the headboard, and made a second guess. "Is it Papa? Didn't he have a gold tooth?"

"He had eight or nine, I think." Emmy shrugged with her awkward matchstick arms. "No, it isn't him. How could it be? I always, always hated Papa. Why should I love him now that he's dead? What is there to love about the dead, except that they're not in your way? What strange ideas you have."

"Well then," Margaret Gloriana snapped. "Who is it, who can it be? There's nobody."

"He's coming." Emmy's eyes had an unsettling starry luster to them, entirely inappropriate for a woman her age. "You'll see."

Margaret Gloriana looked incredulous, wheezed—she couldn't help it. The sound created a brassy vibration in the hollow expanse of the room. Her sister was a ninny, always had been, anyone could see, disrupting their fragile serenity, threatening their sistership with youthful fantasies.

"And when he comes, what will you do with him, you old moth?"

As much as they had seen of life, they had not seen much of men. They were not beauties, but they were not without their feminine merits either. Even so, year after year, they were condemned never to be more to any man's life than their father's maiden daughters, and the island itself conspired with this destiny. Once, on the Queen's birthday, they had both danced the quadrille with a Captain Selcroft, ashore off one of the trading ships, but their father spoiled it by belligerently insisting he be told which one Selcroft intended to marry; and when the Captain balked, challenged him to an affair of honor; and when the Captain refused to raise a pistol on the grounds that the daughters, as fair as they may be, weren't ladies enough to die for—an opinion to which *pere* Parker brutally conceded—challenged him to a horserace, which Selcroft accepted, but finished the loser with a broken neck. Only a Napoleon was foolish enough to fetch away an island girl.

"When he comes, then I shall die . . . and happily," Emmy confessed. She crossed her forearms over the washboard of her ribs as though she were practicing to be stuffed in a hole. "Not a day sooner."

But how unfair, thought Margaret Gloriana, who by virtue of being the elder felt she had every right to die first. Besides, Mary Elizabeth would appreciate the upper hand, late as it was to come to her, and who in the world would tend to her corpse and save her spirit from wandering about if not Emmy.

7

"What shall you die of, then?"

"Is it at all true what they say, that you can die of love?" Emmy whispered in ghostly repose, her hands clasped over her flaccid bosom. "That would be the least I could do for love, after all this time. Wouldn't you think?"

Margaret Gloriana groused for a bit, unimpressed. "You always want everything perfect," she said.

They were without oil lamps or candles but it didn't matter. When the sun, only minutes from setting, dropped into the western windows in the late afternoon, the glare was a powerful soporific; it absorbed their reservoir of strength, disordered their thoughts, and put them almost instantly to sleep: the deepest, most forlorn, most uninhabited sleep they had ever experienced. They were also in the habit of waking hours later, simultaneously, like a pair of zombies, in the middle of the night. Then they would use the chamber pot and patter back to bed, nestled together but trying not to move, listening to the gunfire in the mountains while they waited for their wistfulness to turn to a second, more benevolent sleep. For years (they didn't know how many exactly) the island had been occupied by foreign troops (they didn't know whose, really) and a resistance movement had organized against the outsiders (they weren't actually sure why) but they did know that the men only fought after dark, which the sisters thought cowardly and of a fiendish design. Eventually they would close their eyes again, the translucent lids lowering shut, and enjoy separate but identical dreams: the *vévé* the old black man had scratched in the dirt under the gnip tree, a cross-hatched heart pierced by two swords. Now it was being inscribed by Captain Selcroft.

~

Not the following day but not long after, perhaps a day or perhaps two, Mary Elizabeth was kneeling on the sill of a south window, her insubstantial waist encircled by Margaret Gloriana while she stretched as far as she could—not very far because she was characteristically timid and her sister was making her do it anyway, so her heart wasn't in it—stretching to reach a second group of ripe gnips, the first and closest already eaten in weeks past. Birds dashed from branch to branch with dizzying speed, mocking her. She leaned a few more inches, then for no apparent reason and without warning, Emmy blasted the fresh morning air with one of her girlish screams. Margaret Gloriana hugged tighter—all their lives they had been lean healthy women, not weak (though Maggie was tall), and now they each weighed no more than a basket of sorrel blossoms. She tried to pull Emmy back in but couldn't; her sister spread herself out like a cobweb in the window, opening her knees and grabbing hold of the shutters and vines. "Are you falling?" Margaret Gloriana asked. "You don't seem to be."

Emmy quit resisting and floated in her sister's arms. Margaret Gloriana helped her down quickly from the sill, afraid she was being stung to death by jack spaniars or assaulted by the birds. Once she was on her feet again, Emmy, her face feverish, her jaw quivering, took one guilty glancing look at Margaret Gloriana and burst into tears. She gestured toward the south as if she were shooing mosquitoes.

"There's a man on horseback coming," she wailed miserably.

The older sister rushed to the window. "Where?" There was nothing much wrong with her sight, but she could see no man on horseback near or far.

"He's a white man," blubbered Emmy.

"Impossible," Margaret Gloriana clucked. "Inconceivable. You're making-believe again." She peered into the green-tangled distance where disciplined groves had once stood, as sweet to the eye as rose gardens. Nothing was out there anymore but a spiteful jungle re-creating itself. Not a chicken or peacock or guinea fowl, not a goat or black-bellied sheep, not an ox or cow, a donkey or a horse, and certainly not a backra man, which would be terribly disconcerting, for neither of them had seen or spoken to a white man in years, and they would sooner transform themselves into *crapauds* than prepare for a civilized visit. It was an indecent idea.

"Stop bawling," Margaret Gloriana said, leading her sister back to bed. "It's very tiresome to hear you go on like this. No one's coming." She cuddled her sister to her breast and rocked gently, as she had so many times in the past. Who would come this far into the abandoned countryside to gape at two old women with flesh like salt cod and not a stitch to wear? Who even knew they were alive, and why should anyone care, and if they cared, what business was it of theirs, she'd like to know.

"My lover," lamented Emmy, reading her sister's mind, a skill she had been explicitly forbidden to use long ago. "If only I had some violet water."

"Oh dear, let's not start up with that." Were they even alive? Maybe someone would come and tell them if they were one way or another.

"Or a gown. Or just a ribbon for my hair."

Not much was wrong with the old sisters' hearing either, and they were both startled by the muffled impish laugh of a whinny, still miles away on the serpentine path that traversed down palisades, dipped into ravines, wove through vaulted tunnels of ceiba trees, vanished across irrigation canals grown solid with lily pads—yet close enough to make their hearts flutter. Emmy felt her sister's long nails dig into her shoulders and she squirmed to the other side of the bed.

"I told you," Emmy despaired. "Dear God Almighty Jesus, what shall I wear?" She begged her sister to go back to the window to see how near the rider had come.

"No, I can't bear it." Margaret Gloriana rasped her disavowal of whatever might happen next. She began to shudder and pulled the sheet up to her chin. "I don't want to see a white man. You go."

But Emmy herself was too distraught to move except to yank her own side of the sheet up to her face, so they lay there quaking, their dehydrated skin turned clammy. The horse whinnied again, much nearer, then after a while snorted, nearer still, and not a minute later the day which had been like so many others and not worth complaining about, because what had been done was irreparable—was being praised in a booming voice that seemed to cause a rumble in the stone foundation of the house.

"Good day, good day, good day!"

"I'm fainting," said Emmy in a barely audible sigh.

"So am I," answered Margaret Gloriana. "He's your lover. Tell him to go away."

There was a knocking—though not at the door, for the servants had sprung its hinges and taken it too.

"Hello, halloo, *bonjour,* anybody home?"

"He has a powerful voice," noted Emmy.

"He sounds to me like a *cinquantaine,*" Margaret Gloriana replied, hissing. She had no precise idea of what a *cinquantaine* actually was, only that it was her father's most relished label for whomever he didn't like. He had been a man delighted with the abundance of his enemies— Irish rebels, Gallic Protestants and Papists, Scottish Covenanters, Quakers, Puritans, and all manner of psychotics, convicts, and deportees, not to mention the Dutch, the Portagee, Jacobin French, and barbarous Spaniards. The intruder down below would likely be representing one or more of these diabolic traditions.

"A hairpin," murmured Emmy, "a teaspoon of scented powder."

"If he comes in the house he'll murder us," said Margaret Gloriana. "That's what kind of white men show their face these days."

He came in the house, stamping his boots on the fractured terrazzo, crunching a path through broken table legs and chicken bones and the busted machinery of clocks. They listened to him playing football with coconut husks, they heard the tintinnabulation of porcelain and pottery, shattered on a night of inscrutable liberation. What made them all the more apprehensive was his dreadful whistling, a low-pitched melody like none they had ever imagined, a sinister bold and bumpy rhythm. When he reached the wooden floorboards of the dining hall he became an earthquake, and when a foot thundered down on the first step of the main staircase, and then the second thundered down on the next step, and so on to the top of the landing, the two Miss Parkers whipped the sheet over their heads and lay petrified, immobile as plaster saints. Throughout the halls and passages the repercussing amplified to apocalyptic proportion; he clomped from room to room like a nosy Goliath until at last he clomped into theirs and halted at the foot of the bed. The whistling ceased, but the atmosphere still rang with his noise.

"Are you alive?" he inquired politely.

He repeated the question in Spanish, which confirmed Margaret Gloriana's cutthroat fears, and then in French, which made Emmy shiver imperceptibly in anticipation, because she had always known the French to wear such provocative hats. Receiving no response, the man began to pull ever so cautiously at the sheet, inching it down farther and farther until he saw one grizzled and one flossy mop of hair, pinkish scalps, and the glossy crowns of two foreheads, liver-spotted and additionally marred by the scarlet dappling of sun-made cancers. He took a steadying breath and continued: a double set of eyebrows astonishing for their coal-black thickness, and then, regrettably, the pure but lifeless eyes, wonder-stricken by the beyond. His face saddened, he drew his hand back from the sheet and crossed himself, muttering in a language neither sister could understand. but which sounded like groans and smacks. He went to a window and sagged against its peeling frame, staring out at the vast and savage terrain.

Contained within the slightest exhalation of breath, a sound not different from the natural silence of the house, Mary Elizabeth spoke to her sister.

"He's wonderful."

Margaret Gloriana puffed back, an insufflation as soft as blowing into a baby's ear. "He's much too young—and thin."

"He's very handsome."

"He has a nose like a Jew."

They did not think it odd or offensive that the young man had a carbine strapped across his back, for on the island men had always carried guns, even to the dinner table, and they did not perceive that his soiled gray blouse and stained flannel pants were in fact a uniform. But through the weave of the sheet, Margaret Gloriana, at least, could taste the bitterness of cordite that enveloped him, and smell the familiar sorrow of blood, and knew without having to ask that he had come fresh from battle.

Emmy would have registered this evidence too, for her senses were equally refined by solitude as her sister's, but she was drifting, overwhelmed, pursuing vague memories of passion through the museum of her heart.

~~~

The young deserter went from window to window, surveying the dense panorama, and assured himself he had not been followed. He wished he had discovered the two old women alive and prosperous, quick to offer him a plate of lamb and pudding, and he would sit, assuming they owned a chair, and confess the peculiar fate that had befallen him and they, poor withered figs, saturated with long experience distilled to wisdom of the world, would advise him what to do. They would tell him how to undo what history had done to him: how he, a Flemish village boy who aspired to play in the most renowned beer gardens and cabarets of Europe, lubricating the dreams of the masses with new and dangerous music, how he, who until yesterday had masqueraded as the heroic Charlie Andrews, might recross the ocean and repatriate himself to the ravaged continent as his civilian self, the Liege *savant* by the name of Josef Krunder, who since the age of three could play the *Marseillaise* or any of a dozen anthems on whatever instrument he was handed. He, Josef Krunder, who was Charlie Andrews risen to First Lieutenant's rank, a member of a great army that had been victorious in a great war, now doomed by an invisible momentum to tidy up jungles and deserts, islands with names no one ever heard.

On the other hand, he had participated in splendid adventures, and increased his repertoire of popular songs tenfold—but enough was enough.

LES FEMMES CREOLES

Throughout the exotic diaspora of sinners where he had campaigned, he had viewed uncountable dead, the majority of them flayed and mutilated, and he had stumbled upon more than a few old women like these in the bed, but none so intimately. They were like forsaken goddesses who had outlasted their value, dispossessed by their celebrants and allowed to spoil, unworshipped, suspended in purgatory between a fallen world and one as yet unborn. He returned across the room to replace the sheet as he had found it, taking a last gaze into the soul of their eyes, inanimate as miniature pale-blue doll parasols. Swept by profound homesickness—what, after all, had become of his own mother?—he marched out of the bedroom, downstairs, and then outside into the heat, from a cistern splashed water on his face and neck and began to police the grounds in search of a shovel, obligated by a Christian upbringing to bury the hags before he rode on to the sea.

After a time he gave up the hunt, having discovered nothing in the dilapidated outbuildings of any use save a hoe blade with its shaft broken and a cutlass filed as sleek as a rapier. Back to the house he went, through a rear entrance that passed him into a library strewn with excreta and goose feathers, its remaining volumes flowering a slick vivid mold, and he thought to himself that he would say a prayer over the stiffs and leave it at that. Belated last rites. But the day had progressed too far for traveling hostile territory, and he reasoned he should stop the night until the moon rose, and then go on. His village superstitions, however, argued against such a plan: pass the evening with two dead women and get attached to whatever curse lingered over the violated estate. Yet to think of the world this way, so vulnerable to mystery, was no longer possible for Josef Krunder Charlie Andrews. His conscience chided him, he was taunted by the imperatives of manhood, and so he resolved to stay—and to quicken the time he would offer a requiem, so that the dead might look down from heaven and know they had not been, for once, forgotten.

In the final hour of daylight, the sisters as unconscious as logs, he ascended to the sun-swept upstairs room outfitted like a junk dealer. From the ubiquitous trash of devastation, he had combed three galvanized pails with their bottoms partially rusted out, a length of cedar planking hanging by its last nail from one of the sheds, a half-burnt spindle from a ladder-back chair, and from his saddle an army-issued wool blanket and a paraffin plug of candle. Near the foot of the bed he went to work, set the cedar plank spanning two of the pails, upturned the third as a stool cushioned by folding his blanket into a pad. Out the windows, the evening's stridulation of crickets and frogs began to saw at the tranquility of twilight. He lit the candle and took his seat, gripped the charred point of the spindle, and with it reproduced a crude outline of a keyboard upon the surface of the cedar plank, minus the highest and lowest scales for want of space. He flexed his hands, practiced several finger exercises, limbering the knuckles, and called the notes in his head but to his surprise they came as sterile letters, not tones, until he pictured the clefs like a charge of helmeted troops, advancing through the scales from bass to treble.

His countercharge, the requiem. He was ready to perform.

"Eternal rest grant upon them, O Lord," he sang in a tenor's voice. His spidery hands crept along the board in a solemn cadence, the calluses tweaked by splinters, fingertips blackened by char. His amateurish preoccupation with striking the correct keys; a panic as the formal sequence of the mass temporarily faded from memory—these shortcomings slowly dissolved and he was transported by the

literal resurrection, impoverished as it was, of music. As his instincts revived and intensified, he concentrated less on the act itself and more on abstract appreciation, oneness, union. He smiled mournfully upon his subjects, aware that they and they alone could hear the divine orchestration that resonated with such compassion within the chamber of his mind, but as he approached the *Dies Irae,* he was spontaneously delivered back to his youth into the slicing scrubbed hands of his choirmaster father, a bloody bastard he was, and he inhaled again the frankincense of suffocation of the church, and felt its smothering robes on his shoulders. His hands slammed clumsily on the plank, he glowered at the two desiccated crones and their whiffy mattress, his eyes raked their loathsome morbid shapes. And as he played on, his nails indenting the wood, he realized something was different—wrong—about the arrangement of the corpses. He squinted through the dim and shifting illumination, his voice rose until he was bellowing in Latin. The noise outside the windows churned like the engines of a mighty factory. Was he mad, or had the geometry of their bones been reformulated? Then he had it: When he had first looked down upon them earlier in the day, they were aligned in bed like two fallen fence posts in a snowy field. Now they had thaumaturgically branched. Now their parallel arms formed a chevron. They were holding hands.

"The hell with this, ladies," Charlie Josef sang, and with a flourish of vaudevillian chords, bridged over to a ragtime dirge, putting himself in a sweat. Then he gave the two possums love songs, folk songs, drinking songs, ballads from operettas, every music-hall ditty that came to mind, songs in Flemish and Celtic, Finnish and German, torch songs, war songs, minstrel songs and shanties, verse upon verse, chorus and refrain, one after another on into the night until his mouth was paste and his throat nostalgically raw, the candle extinguished to a frozen puddle and the room flooded with satin mists of moonlight.

With throbbing fingers and stiffness in his knees, his thighs cramped from riding all last night, down from the mountains, he got to his feet, refastened his rifle over his shoulder, and approached the head of the bed. Tenderly, he turned back the corner of the sheet, exposing Mary Elizabeth's smitten expression, and bent over.

"How far is the coast, madame?"

"Two leagues southwest," peeped Emmy to the relief of Margaret Gloriana, who was sure her sister had fulfilled her own premonition by dying hours ago when she had released her water into the mattress, and her hand had gone limp and cool. Still, she didn't think it necessary to converse with the man in French, like a soubrette. He leaned over and turned the opposite corner of the sheet, but Margaret Gloriana clung to inexpression, refuting any notion of her continued existence.

"Can I do something for you, *Gran-mere?*"

Emmy asked that he send her a pair of black crepe drawers, if he'd be so kind.

~~~

She remained in an ecstatic trance for days, effervescing upon occasion, uttering endearments at the birds, fragmented lyrics, frivolities about gold teeth (which she hadn't verified) and artistic temperament, until Margaret Gloriana was disgusted with her pretense, the latest of many perpetrated by her younger sister since they were children. She contrived a list of mortal sins the singer had most likely committed in his young life, but Emmy wouldn't listen, and so in frustration over losing her company, she fought fire with fire and declared that she too had a lover.

In Emmy's eyes, the cloudy bliss instantly clarified, her nostrils dilated with the restorative vapors of rivalry. "Why, I don't believe it," she protested. "I would be so happy for you, but I don't believe it at all."

"Yes," Margaret Gloriana held firm, although she herself didn't believe a word that rolled from her mouth, "and he will come very very soon."

"How do you know? Can't you tell him there's no hurry?"

Emmy felt her sister meant to punish her for luring the singer to Derby Hill with her yearning. Ever since his nocturnal concert, all Margaret could do was malign his innocent talents, point to the smudged board across the pails (which she dare not touch) as if it were a pagan altar, diminish the gift he had endowed to her memory. He sang such devilish things, Margaret Gloriana accused daily. Oh, they were so much fun, Emmy would defend. His intention was to rob all that was left in the house, and that could only be their eternal spirits, her older sister retorted. But that was fine with Emmy; she said he was welcome to hers.

"I know because the shooting has stopped at night." The end of the conflict seemed to have occurred the evening before the white man appeared to beguile them with evil crooning. "The war is over," Margaret Gloriana improvised. "He has done his duty valiantly. He is free. I won't say another word about it."

They lay together at a standstill for several more days, fatigued by the smallest exchange of civilities encouraged by this new tension. They sucked on the creamy orange pulp of gnips, sipped cistern water from cracked cups, and tried to speak of other less selfish things. Of their mother, for instance, who became ill when they were twelve and six and returned to her homeland for treatment. They could not remember the illness she suffered, but the treatment administered apparently had great healing power, for it cured her of being a colonist's wife.

"She sent for us and sent for us," recalled Emmy.

"But she died."

"Father wouldn't agree."

"But he did. We couldn't leave, though, unless she came to claim us."

"She never came."

"She couldn't. He would have hacked her to pieces."

"Would you have gone?"

Their remembrance of their mother consistently ended with this uncomfortable question, each of them shy to answer for fear of distressing the other, and they would move on to other events.

"The November hurricane was the worst day of my life."

"It killed Alexander Brumfield." Emmy threw a gnip seed at a trio of grackles on the sill.

"You were too young to remember."

"I remember. The servants picked cuttlefish out of the trees."

"Alexander was cut right in half. Something flew in the air and hit him, but it went so fast no one saw what it was."

"Alexander was going to marry you."

"You can't remember, you were only three."

"I was four. The fishermen never came home, but their boats did. I remember we made coffins from them."

The sisters conjured up the scouring stones along the river bank, the eddies of moss-green water. The stones were flipped like pancakes during an earthquake and ruined for laundering for at least another century, their smooth lye-bleached surfaces, burnished by so much cotton, replaced by slime-coated coarse undersides. The same catastrophe had rocked the Virgin Mary from her chapel pedestal, breaking the statue into three pieces and releasing an egg snake that had lived in the hollow of the casting. Their father had it caught, and kept in a grass basket on a table in the parlor, and only white men were permitted to look at it. The sisters saw the workers in the fields fanned out like a line of ragged infantry, bent to the ground in a torturous advance, as if searching all day for a dropped coin. And the painter from Italy who resembled, in their opinion, a Biblical shepherd. The servant women were rendered too merry and independent by his brush, with faces like voluptuous moons, and no one purchased the canvases. They reminisced about the itinerant professor, his smokehouse pungency; his thin frock coat, his mustard shirt with too few buttons, the gray trousers with a black stripe down the outer seams; his green flat-sided carpenter's pencil; his purse a soda-cracker tin with a rope strap, stuffed with papers. He left them untutored except through mimicry, scattered lines from *Othello* and *The Tempest*—"Hell is empty, and all the devils are here" and "Do that good mischief which may make this island thine own forever"—and schooled them in the details and habits of foreigners, a class that excluded no one. They remembered the dentist in the capital who repaired their teeth with caulking compound; the charcoal-makers who cooked entire trees like pigs in the soil; the vomit smell of grinding houses and the caramel smell of boiling houses; the taste of the baked spheres of cheeses, stuffed with prawns, sweetbreads, and pigeons; tamarind butter, sunbonnets, and whale oil lamps; the vulgar little monkeys that would shit on the veranda; the parrots, now extinct, and the carnival flamboyance of their plumage.

The campfires of the laborers, the ululation of their legends. How many empty columns of time had passed since they had admired the handsomeness of their father's *paso finos,* the best of them raced in Jamaica? And before the instrument was outlawed by the last governor, the frantic seductive sound of the *tambu,* drumming from inside the mountains? Neither of them could say how many years it had been since the week-long poisoning epidemic, which first took their father's bulls, then his mastives, then the man himself; they could remember the last drought because of the pink-and-black-petaled strawflowers that bloomed only during periods of exceptional dryness. And they could hear their mother teaching them the alphabet as if they had savored the queer vinegary edge of her breath—she drank red wine—only yesterday:

A is for Albion; B is for Berkshire and Buckingham; C is for the Crown and Cruelty; D is for Devonshire, Drake, Decadence, and the Damned; and E is for Eternity, which is the length of any day under this roof.

But the alphabet failed to subvert the sisters. Their mother could not persuade her daughters that they were prisoners in a world confounded by an inexhaustible capacity for sin; she could not teach them not to call it home.

⁓

And so he came, as he must given the unwitting prescience of the sisters, the thinning of the veil stretched across the future. He was one of the freedom fighters, a black man come out of the mountains after untold years of struggle. He hung with filthy rags; one leg bled from an undressed wound, and the flesh around his left eye was slack from an invisible injury. There were no more bullets for the rifle he carried, but he didn't need them anyway for he had triumphed over his enemies, over all adversity, and was now untouchable. He limped through the broad shadows of waning moonlight. With eyes most keen after sundown, he inspected the *vévé* at the base of the gnip tree; other signs throughout the yard—the skeleton of a land turtle, an erebus moth that flew against his cheek—warned him that Derby Hill was haunted. But he knew as well already, it was why he had come, and he praised the gods for this opportunity, this further evidence that he had been chosen, that his trials were divine, that now he must wage peace on the dead as successfully as he had waged war on the living. He had returned to his place of birth.

The two old sisters, in between their first and second sleep, heard the sawboning of the jungle cease and knew he had arrived, passing over the grounds and into the house with no more disturbance than a stray breeze rising off the sea. They listened carefully and for some time heard nothing, nothing distinct other than the tremulous presence of his breathing in the kitchen, until finally there was an anguished cry, and the house echoed with his grieving.

"Why does he weep?" Mary Elizabeth asked in a whisper.

"Oh, how should I know?" Margaret Gloriana said, acutely agitated. She wanted this fellow to come up, present himself with expedience, then go about his business elsewhere. She was feeling especially old and frail tonight, weary of this recent plague of males, tipping the sublime calibration of the scales of sisterhood. Nevertheless, she felt compelled to defend him. "And why shouldn't he weep?" she said. "It's no worse than the other one's singing."

Yet it was worse, much worse, this tragic outpour, and it resounded through the ruin of the house and into the surrounding countryside like the mourning of a nation. "I wouldn't say he's terribly pleased to be here," Emmy observed.

"Quick to judge, quick to apologize." Her sister lowered herself off her elbows.

There was a natural rhythm to his baritone keening; before long the sisters had accustomed themselves to its aqueous surges, its failing ebbs, and were lulled back into their twin dreams of Captain Selcroft. They woke at dawn to the same sobs, which had lost none of their vigor. All through the day the man's marathon sorrow continued unabated, afflicting the two old Miss Parkers with its depth of wretchedness and preempting their sisterly discussions, but as the sun balled its light and simmered down toward the western windows, the crying stopped and Emmy, who was first to see him enter the bedroom, made a ravenous gasp for air as if she had been submerged underwater and had almost drowned. Thus alerted, Margaret Gloriana sat up in bed and, mortified by what she saw, just as quickly slumped back down.

"That's not who you think it is!" she blurted out.

"Mother of God," said Emmy, "you're in love with a darkie." So much of the time through the years there had been scant else to do but look in the opposite direction, not merely away from the tribulations of the blacks, but from the extravagances of the whites as well, and half the world was too full of wonder, the other half constricted by manners and taboos, to have extra room for temptation. And so Mary Elizabeth marveled at how impetuous her sister had become at the end of her life.

Margaret Gloriana, however, was hardly capable of speaking. "Absolutely not," she croaked without her customary authority. "That's his servant." But she knew this was no more true than her original announcement, that this feral being poised inside the door was no more another man's servant than he was or could be her swain, real or imagined, if at all a man himself, and yet despite his lycanthropic eyes and beard, and the mien of a beast who feasted on human virtues, from the sound of it he had wept as other men do, with a crushed heart, a long-suffering spirit, and a lust for the infancy of pain. In this regard his humanity was more outspokenly noble than their father's ever had been, their father who had lived in a closet of avarice and moral certainty and had died roaring hatred for all peoples, including his own kind. Still, Margaret Gloriana surmised, she had stupidly, childishly, summoned a nemesis, the only lover that would ever come for either sister—the brilliant solitaire, their death.

As for the black maroon, whose name was Alvaro Toussaint Parker—no blood relation but the surname of a slave brand inherited from his ancestors—he took one freezing look at the sisters, the prominence of their yellowing teeth, the transparent skin varnished around their skulls, the witch's locks, the purpled eyepits, the beaks of nose, and addressed them as if they were indeed already dead, though of a more privileged caste of duppy than the other ghosts he had sought to communicate with during his time in the house. Falling to his knees at their bedside, he spoke to the spirits as a supplicant.

"I might ask you to ask my mother to forgive me," he said.

Straight off, the sisters were too amazed by the formality and dignified tone of his speech to reply. He had mastered their own language, the house language and empire's language, but emitted from so swollen a mouth it struck their ears as a masquerade, a subterfuge. It so spun around Emmy's thoughts that she changed roles and responded in the patois that was or should have been his own, maintaining a most irregular social symmetry.

"Hear now, Moses, who you muddah?" she squeaked and, aghast, clapped her hand over her mouth.

Margaret Gloriana yawned, willing herself to remain composed, yet she began to feel drowsy. "Why don't you go on your way and ask her yourself?" she suggested. She blinked uncontrollably and yawned a second time.

"My mother was Lydalia Parker, laundress," Alvaro Toussaint Parker answered the first sister. Throughout the past infelicitous hours he had spent in the house, that's all he had done: asked his mother directly for forgiveness for betraying his eight brothers and four cousins by conspiring with the occupation troops, because you can persuade yourself of many crimes when you know you cannot win, nor your cause prevail, and so he had led his comrades into ambush. All night and all day he had offered contrition, beseeched his mother for absolution. Instead of acknowledging him, she would not come away from her scouring stones at the river, where she slapped massa's wet linens against the whitened boulders, kneading them like dough with her muscular arms, singing hymns of resurrection. He felt he would go mad begging her to come to her feet and comfort him, her youngest son, in his grim passage of leadership.

"Lydalia Parker, laundress," he droned balefully, "Lydalia Parker, mother of her country."

Lydalia's family *was* big, I recall, thought Emmy as she sank into unconsciousness. He bowed his leaf-flecked head to wait for the dead to deliver his penance, craving pardon so that he might resume his self-appointed mission without malediction. He remained kneeling, full of remorse; the sisters fondly remembered the laundress Lydalia Parker but had ceded the power to speak; the western windows blazed like doors thrown open to a hellish furnace. Blood-red glorioles irradiated the phantoms in the bed; Alvaro raised his eyes and saw the spirits reduce glimmer by shrinking glimmer back into nothingness of inert flesh. In the deluded mind of Alvaro Toussaint Parker, their departure was a merciless disconnection. The *loas* had rejected his plea, they would not enter as his advocate into the netherworld and intervene on his behalf. He bounded to his feet, vowing this was the first and last time he would petition backra spirits for their charity. He noticed the cedar plank on its pails, deciphered its smudges, and Alvaro Toussaint Parker condemned himself for not foreseeing the full and malicious range of plots he was up against. He crawled from the house, on hands and knees, sideways at times like a crab, to search for his mother's grave.

They awakened at their habitual hour, in the middle of the night, not to the distant pops of gunfire, or the chirring of the insects, but this time to the labor of muffled chopping, and they rose together, Ladies Lazarus, and went to stand in the northern windows. There was another, more fluid sound reaching them, like blankets being shaken out, and now they located its source, the high fire on the nearby hillside within the low stone walls of Derby Hill's cemetery. The shape of a man jerked between flame and shadow, lifting an arm, a skull balanced in its hand.

"It's the professor," Emmy said. He had been given to campfire reenactments of *Hamlet,* staged on the dirt between the cluster of servants' huts.

"What's he doing back, do you think?" Margaret Gloriana wondered—out loud or to herself, it no longer mattered.

27

"I suppose no one told him that everything's different now."

Hand in hand the sisters wobbled back to bed a last time.

Alvaro Toussaint Parker dropped the skull of his laundress mother into the conflagration, gathered the leathery scales of her skin, the kindling of her bones, and threw them in as well. He withdrew from the plot of his ancestors and slunk farther up the hill to its crest and renewed his digging, sinking the hoe blade with the broken shaft at a furious pace, as far into the rich ground as he could drive it. *Go on,* he heard the sisters urge in their transcended voices, and he struck open the old patriarch's coffin and cast his poison-twisted bones into the flames. *Go on,* the sisters urged through the night, *Go on,* as he persevered, emptying grave after grave, until by dawn he had spent his obsession, tarred by mud and ash and crumbs of dead peoples' clothes, and there was but one grave undisturbed in the cemetery, its marker carved with a sailing ship.

"Go on," exhorted Margaret Gloriana in the black man's ear. "That one too."

"Him especially," said Mary Elizabeth.

With all the strength of those before him who had been bonded to the land, Alvaro Toussaint Parker obeyed this ultimate command and hoed as long as it took to finish the job of enthrallment forever. Then, exhausted, he stumbled to the river, past the scouring stones with their dark sides turned up, stripped the abomination of rags from his body, and washed himself. Energy crackled back into his flesh and he returned to the grounds of the manor house and stood below the gnip tree, adorning himself with peddler's jewels. Naked but for these cast-off ornaments of his destiny, he reentered the shambles of the house and mounted the stairs, wrapped his waist with the threadbare sheet, tore the sleeves from the muslin nightgown and dropped it over his head like a vestment, and descended once more to the outside world to begin his long arduous pilgrimage across the island, to the capital where he would rule his people in the lunatic passions popular to this day, leaving the two old Miss Parkers curled on the mahogany bed of their parents, the windows filled with curious grackles, the *vévé* cleaned away by the advent of the rains, a graveyard readied for the future, the sisters hand in hand with expressions isolated from possibility but as if poised to fall faithfully under the influence of an irresistible attraction.

STOLEN KISS

On an inside day in November, a smoke and cider day, Burton Glass found a white greasy kiss stamped against the black post of the sun porch he was painting at the shore, off-season in Rehobeth.

It pleased him. Look at that, he said.

He worked facing the sea, which today was friendless, dulled by empty grandeur and an early winter. He saw only where his brush pointed, where the textures changed. In the cold his hands were dumb animals, struggling and stupid, pushing against their task. He wanted them to be stronger, to remember a better day, remember a woman or a fire. His leather gloves made him feel clumsy, so he took them off after the first few strokes.

Behind the DuPont place up the beach the geese on Silver Lake cried: the unmusical chorus, the tock of migrating wings, the splash of the spinning gadwalls and pintails on the restful water. The noise came across the dunes to Burton as if there were no distance between the lake and the porch, and it comforted in a powerful way and kept him company.

Burton finished the south post and moved over to the middle one, starting at the base. The darkly stained wood was dry, saturated with salt, rough but not splintering. He pecked at it with his brush, stooping to also take his pipe from where he'd set it on the deck. Too much of the season came through into his lungs as he sucked the cold stem. The ash was dead and bitter. He paused to relight it, gazing out along the strand. The sea was pocked, coarse like steel wool, full of dimension. As he concentrated on the match, a wave rose above the tidal slope, held up by the wind and feathered backward, splitting to the sand. He turned back to the post. Half the way up there was the kiss, circled by a glossy halo of oil that seeped out from the image.

Burton examined the mark. He had not expected such a thing. Tamping the lid back on the bucket of paint, he squatted down on it to meditate, to smoke his rum-flavored blend. He could not readily come up with anything to think about, then recalling it was the kiss that stopped him, Burton dreamed a little about the private act of a woman, into August and blood-hot air, skin blistered beyond appeasement but finally soothed by cream and lotion, smeared onto the face, over red cheeks and burnt lips. Little wordless dreams saying nothing, just feelings and fragrances that pushed their blessed way through into the day.

This was not his house. He rarely had talked with the women—mother and daughter—who weekended here, both dark haired, distant bodies he had stared at on the beach, admiring how much they might have given or how much more they could. The husband was a lawyer from

New York. As caretaker, Burton received his check, carelessly inscribed, and the checks of many others—lawyers, bankers, businessmen—on the first of each month. The mail had no immediacy for Burton anymore. For the past year he only made bi-weekly visits to the post office—once for the money, and once to collect the letter from his own wife, who still lived in the Washington suburbs. She was faithful in her writing. Her letters usually arrived the second week of each month. They were chatty and honest and full of little news. Burton enjoyed reading them as a diversion.

Maybe it was the fellow's wife, Burton thought, looking again at the kiss. She seemed happier when her husband didn't come down with her and the girl. There was never that forced gaiety about her, never the staged manners; even the clothes she wore were more casual and free when the man wasn't there. But Burton could not discount the daughter. The source of the kiss might have indeed been her. He had seen how her breasts and hips had grown in the past two or three years, how the boys had found her out there on the sand, sometimes had heard the faint, wonderful language she used, at night in the dunes, as she marked her discoveries. She shrieked once when his dog surprised them back there; Burton heard a young man's voice bringing the girl back into his arms. It was easy to love these things about people he did not know, but he couldn't look at his own life like that. After thirty-two years in Washington, it was hard to see what was genuine and what was not. You had to decompress after being down into it for so long, the *it* a state of affairs not unlike the cold mud shore around the lake, gray and smelling of decay, an airless trap. He had sat behind his desk all those years knowing he was in the wrong place. The beach became his tonic. To now work with one's hands, to scrape and callus them, to be next to the sea when everyone else had abandoned it, to preside over quiet cottages full of the lives of others—this was good, this made sense, to see and feel what you do.

Burton arose from the bucket, a familiar pain soaking his legs, to stand before the kiss. The lips of the woman or girl had set a perfect print. He touched the surface. It did not smear; the wood had taken it in, would hold the kiss forever in sterile ownership. He leaned out over the rail of the porch to knock the crumbs and dust from his pipe.

This was enough for now. Burton wanted something in his belly, a nugget or flame that would warm his blood. He cleaned out the brush so it would be ready for his return, passed through the French doors directly into the master bedroom—her bedroom. Usually he would keep going, but he stopped this time to turn up the thermostat. When he finished the porch he must work in here, replace a closet door. The bed was quilted, the pillows uncased. He saw small things he'd never bothered to notice before: a clean ashtray made from a cockle shell, a blue fountain pen and bottle of pills on the night table, a metallic tube of lipstick on the dresser next to a hand mirror. Why, he did not know, he could not tell himself, he had never done a thing like this, but he slid open the top drawer of the dresser—nothing. He opened another—bobby pins and ribbons, a tortoise-shell clasp. In the next one down were sheets, linen pillow cases, army blankets. The bottom drawer—two sweaters, lemon and pink, a folded nightgown, and a bra, the elastic in its straps warped from many washings, so many doings and undoings. Burton picked it up, held it, brought it to his nose to smell—ah, so clean. There was a slow, nervous thrill that came from the silken touch. Before replacing it next to the gown, he held each cup in his palms and imagined the breasts that once filled those crumpled, unshaped spaces.

STOLEN KISS

Taking the stairs down to the first level, he left the house, walking up the beach toward town. The lake was visible between the dunes, the noisy congregations of waterfowl, squadrons circling above, constant arrivals and departures. Not long ago he'd had a good dog, an Irish setter, and the dog died there in the lake. He didn't want to think about it.

The boardwalk began just past the DuPont place. Burton stepped up on it, into more wind, his high-laced boots booming down on the wood, the wind harmless against his stiff white hair trained since boyhood into three patrician waves that rolled straight back from his crown. His wife once said—it was soon after the war— she said, Burton, when you take off your clothes and stand the way you are now, turned just a bit around from the way you're going, you look so handsome and hard. It's your hair, I think, you have the best head of hair, and your nose and the color of your body. How did you get so tan all over? What did you do there in Italy? What was it like? You don't know how much I missed you.

I can imagine, he had answered, but in fact he rarely thought about her when he was over there.

The love between them lasted a long time, longer than he thought it would. It was still there, although they couldn't live together anymore. At least they hadn't used each other up to the point where they wanted nothing, where any desire wasn't worth the effort. It seemed to get that way at times—those middle years when they managed their love as if it were an anemic bank account. Now those days were over. Thank God for letting us be apart and at peace with the loneliness.

His eyes watered in the wind, his chest tightened under the woolen Pendleton. Onto Atlantic Avenue, he passed the shuttered guest houses, the pew-like rows of benches that faced back toward the ocean, the statue of angry Neptune, a lone bicycler in scarf and stocking cap. Inside the Sportsmen's Tavern, his eyeglasses fogged as he moved instinctively toward the first empty stool at the bar. He took a paper napkin to wipe his glasses clean, saw the blurred shape of Carl approaching.

"Burton."

"What?"

The proprietor ambled the length of the counter, stopped to remove a bottle of whiskey from the shelf, and then stood opposite Burton, pouring both of them a shot.

"Your wife called looking for you."

"She leave a message?" The whiskey brought back everything the wind had taken from him.

"She said to tell you that John Warner's left Liz for her. They're running off together."

"What, again?"

"Hah!"

"What did Carole want?"

"She says she can't make it this weekend and she hopes you won't mind. Somebody gave her a ticket to an opening at the Kennedy Center. She said call her back if there's a problem. You want something to eat?"

"If there's chowder, I'll have that."

After he returned from the kitchen and set the steaming bowl in front of Glass, Carl came out from behind the bar to sit. The two men had known each other for many years. Burton sipped the liquid delicately from his spoon.

"Get a new pup yet?" Carl asked.

"No."

"A fellow up in Henlopen has a setter bitch that just had pups. You should have a look."

"All right. Maybe this weekend."

"Rachel was a fine dog. Going to be hard to replace her, Burton."

"Good dog, sure. Dumb though. Rather not have a dog it if can't stand up to a goose."

They had debated the point several times since it happened. Burton said the dog got into the lake, chasing the fowl back and forth, finally swam into an army of Canadians that converged on her. Carl insisted the dog was just old, too old to swim that much, and a goose would be shy of a dog anyway. Red-haired Rachel must have drunk salt water and drowned, in Carl's opinion. Burton no longer cared how it happened, he wouldn't have another dog. Next time it would be the dog that was left behind, can't leave a stupid dog behind.

He stared into his bowl. The milky chowder was the same color as the kiss he had discovered on the porch post. "Carl," he began but stopped himself. He was going to tell about the kiss but thought better of it because when the words started to form they felt like a betrayal, like blabbing about the most intimate moments shared with somebody.

"What?" asked Carl.

"The chowder's good. It's what I needed."

He thought about Rachel. Can't have another dog, but maybe I should. Maybe that's the way my wife is feeling. She didn't put up any fuss. She said, Burton, I've known for a long time that's what you wanted, but I can't spend the rest of my life up there. It's too quiet for me. I can't fit into a place like that after living in a city that has everything. That's too much to ask, but you go on. I'll spend the summers there with you. The summers are good. And we'll visit each other, like lovers. That's the only way I can do it.

"You all right?" Carl asked. "You're not getting a cold, are you?"

"No."

"Another whiskey?"

"No, I'll be getting back now."

———

He stretched out on her bed and watched it happen, let the breeze turn warm again, the heat invade the day. He had a vision of her out there on the sand. She has tried to read her book but cannot focus; the words rise and recede on the page, throb behind her eyes, enter into her as some unintelligible force. She falls asleep on her towel and is unbothered. When she wakes she feels as if she has lost all privacy, that she has been possessed too much, too long, too hard, and every movement now brings pain.

The house is quiet, empty. Her husband never comes with her anymore. The girl is somewhere else, in town parading the boardwalk maybe. The woman enters the room. Although she is still beautiful, still unaged, her face looks battered and blank, untouchable. She carefully removes her top and Burton is startled by her white breasts, so white they no longer seem to belong to the rest of her body. An elegant, enameled fingertip tests the sore red line that vees to the middle of her chest. Her nipples exaggerate the touch. The tight pressure of her skin makes the woman grimace.

Burton thought that now her husband might come and provide a motive for the kiss. He kept still and watched.

But she remains alone despite the expectation that Burton felt in the room. Her hair is swollen and scattered, lightened softly in places where the sun held, where it slowly branded her. Her abdomen is stretched taut, a small, dimpled drum, smoldering underneath the surface. Legs, arms, and cheeks flame brilliantly, her lips pouted and raw as if they have been roughly, persistently, kissed. She twists the lid from a blue jar. Feverish and dizzy, she sinks her fingers into the cream, digging round and round. There is a burning that feels as if it drains her. She stands before the French doors looking out upon the water. Burton saw the strap lines on her back like perfect cuts where her torso had been separated by the sun. Below the horizon, the moon begins paddling the ocean, stroke by stroke across the shadowed water. The woman steps from bedroom to porch, bending down to draw down the bottom of her suit, the clear unsunned flesh unnaturally luminescent, almost transparent, in the dying light. She rubs the cream onto her scorched body, where it melts and sucks the coolness from the rising moon. Standing before the sea, she opens herself to this redemption and sways gratefully, one hand clutching the middle post, pressing her creamed lips against the wood.

Burton paused to study the lines, the ridges and cracks, the thin black space between full halves, this language of the past season, another life. He had loved his wife, Carole, through thirty-nine years, four children and as many homes, a career that seemed more vague with each new day away from it, and now this, their negotiated freedom.

He dipped his brush into the fresh black paint and looked again at the white kiss in the middle of the post. It spoke so much for love when all else tried to ignore it. He traced a finger along the outline, withdrawing his hand finally with irritation. He thought he heard a phone ring somewhere and stopped to listen. It was only the tide coming in, rattling shells together in the trough at land's end. Burton stepped forward and kissed the kiss, glancing to see how closely his lips matched those on the wood. Then he painted over it.

WHERE PELHAM FELL

Less than a year after Colonel Taylor Coates had been told not to drive, he was behind the wheel again, smoking Chesterfields, another habit he had been warned not to pursue, clear-headed and precise in his own opinion, holding to the patriotic speed limit north on Route 29 away from Culpeper in a flow of armies and horses and artillery across the battlefields of Virginia. On one flank the landscape pitched toward a fence of blue mountains, on the other it receded through the bogs and level fields of Tidewater, and as far as Colonel Coates was concerned, there was no better frame for a gentleman's life. There never had been, there never would be, which wasn't just a guess, because the Corps of Engineers had made him world-sore, a forty-year migrant before they discharged him in the direction of the Piedmont.

The confederate John Mosby came onto the road at the Remington turnoff and galloped alongside the car for a mile or two, spurring his Appaloosa stallion. The Colonel decelerated to keep in pace. Mosby pointed to a field map clutched in the same hand that held the reins. His boots were smeared with red clay, the tails of his longcoat flapped, and he held his head erect, his beard divided by the wind. Colonel Coates rolled down the car window and shouted over into the passing lane. *You!* Mosby arched an eyebrow and tapped an ear with his map, leaning to hear the Colonel's voice in the thunder of a diesel truck poised to overtake them. The breeze flipped the Colonel's walking hat into the passenger seat, exposing the white brambles of his hair, blew cigarette ash into his eyes. *That coat you're wearing,* he said, pointing. *Your grandson honored me with a button from the cuff.* The Gray Ghost, as Mosby was known to those who loved or feared him, saluted and rode off onto the shoulder of the pike. The truck rumbled past between them, followed by a long stream of gun caissons pulled by teams of quarter horses showering froth into the air.

Well now, in the presence of consecrated ground even the imaginations of simple men are stirred to hazy visions, and Colonel Coates wasn't simple, only old, recuperating from the shingles and a number of years of puzzling spiritual fatigue, having been given too many years on earth. Brandy Station, two miles south of Elkwood, was where Colonel Coates really headed when he deserted his slumbering wife to replenish the supply of dog food at home, a legitimate errand that he automatically forgot in favor of cruising Fleetwood Hill. The hill was the field of war that engaged him most thoroughly, for there was fought the greatest cavalry battle ever on American soil. The site, virtually unchanged since the mayhem of 1863, had the smell of clover and apple blossoms at this time of year, a nostalgic blend that floated a man's thoughts through the decades of Aprils he'd survived. The Colonel studied accounts of the conflict, knew its opposing strategies, its advances and countercharges, flankings and retreats. He preferred to sit atop a granite outcropping on the knob of the rise and, with an exhilarating rush of details, play out the twelve-hour struggle for himself, the harsh sputtering rake of the enfilades, the agonizing percussion of hooves, swords, musketry. Here the sons of America had devoured one another as if they were Moors and Christians. Here slaughter within the family was an exquisite legend. History could be scratched by the imagination and made to bleed on a few hundred acres of greensward and farmland fouled magnificently by violence.

Almost a year without independence had made Colonel Coates lust for a prowl at Brandy Station. After the war between North and South, that was all the aristocracy had left, the right to remembrance. Taylor had claimed this right and felt obliged to it; his vigil registered in the bloody heart of the land as if he himself—his existence—were the true outcome of the fray: a florid, half-bald man alone in a rolling pasture, hitching his loose pants up repeatedly to keep them above the horns of his failing hips, stricken by the deep blue plunge of loss for those things he wanted but now knew he would not have; for those things he possessed and loved but whose time was past; for myth and time itself, for what was, for the impossibility of ever being there.

And yet he would return from the battlefield uplifted.

Out on the road, however, the Colonel was distracted by the withdrawal of federal troops back across the Rappahannock, and he bypassed Brandy Station, not realizing his mistake until he spotted the marker post commemorating Pelham on the east side of the highway. Major John Pelham commanded Stuart's Horse Artillery until he fell at the battle of Kelly's Ford, mortally wounded by shrapnel that ribboned his flesh and broke the forelegs of his sorrel mount. The skirmish was between cavalry charging blindly through a terrain of deep woods and dense scrub along the banks of the river, the riders cantering through trackless forest, squads of men blundering into tangled thickets, the legs of their coarse pants cut by lead and briar thorns. Down went Pelham as he inspired his men forward, and the event was memorialized many years later by a roadside marker at a junction on Route 29, erected near Elkwood by the United Daughters of the Confederacy, informing the curious that four miles to the southeast the young major had been martyred to the rebel cause.

Abruptly and without signaling, the Colonel veered to the shoulder and turned onto the country road, grim but unrepentant of the nuisance he made for the traffic behind him. Before the privilege of mobility had been taken from him, he had spent one afternoon in aggravated search for the location of Pelham's slaying. The direction of the marker was vague—four miles to the southeast—and the road that supposedly went there split, forked, crossed, and looped through pine and hayfields without bringing Taylor to the ford of the river. Sixteen miles later he threw up his hands and jogged west, eventually arriving at a surfaced pike that returned him to Route 29.

It was now or never again, the Colonel rationalized. From the diaries of the generals he had learned that an opportunity renewed by destiny could not be prevented. The soldiers themselves often hastened forth under the influence of such patterns through the same geography, wandering here and there until suddenly foes met and clashed. The paths they followed were subject to mortifying change. What was right yesterday might be wrong today. But that was the nature of rebel territory—a free-for-all. The Colonel, in slow reconnaissance, took the road to a T intersection, craning to see the houses at the end of their lanes, under a guard of oaks, evergreens, railfences. Virginia, he thought, was the abattoir of the South, mother of the destruction. These were the estates that sent their young men to war, the houses where the lucky wounded returned to expire, where the enemy plundered, where the secessionist ladies wept through the night as the armies marched by. What did people in the North know of the residue of terror that had settled in the stones and beams of these estates? Where in America were there such noble structures, one after another after another, league after league, each a silent record of strife and defeat? It was not an exaggeration to say that the Colonel adored these houses.

At the intersection the pavement ended and an orangeish gravel lane ran left and right. Taylor calculated a southeast direction by examining the sun. The odometer had advanced three miles. He swung left, pleased that the road soon curved, auspiciously by his reckoning, to the south, over swampy ground created, he was sure, by its proximity to the river. For four miles more the road wormed through this low, wet countryside reeking of bog rot, switched its designation twice, and then ascended to higher land, no river in sight, no water crossing, no defunct millhouse, no aura of hostility, nothing but the warm hum of springtime.

By God, I'm missing in action, the Colonel thought, confused as to his whereabouts. And that was how he met President Trass and ended up in possession of the bones.

Cresting a ridge, he sighted the glint of running water a half mile in the distance. The road he was on went off away from it, but there was a narrower track burrowing through a strand of hardwood that appeared as though it might drop in the right direction. On the opposite fringe of the grove, the Colonel saw he had blundered onto private property—and a trash haven at that. The track wasn't a road at all but a drive dead-ending in ruts around an unpainted frame house, the center of a cluster of shanty-like outbuildings and rusted junk. An ancient pink refrigerator stood sentry on a swayback porch, the only color in the monotony of gray and weather-hammered boards. A hound scrambled from under the foundation and barked an alarm. Colonel Coates tried to reverse back through the woods, but he wasn't up to such a maneuver. The rear wheels went off the packed dirt into a spongy muck at the same time the front fender debarked the trunk of a hickory tree. The station wagon lodged across the track, the Colonel demoralized and flustered.

It must be understood that the Colonel was not a man who was unaware, who had no insight into his behavior. He knew full well that he was becoming more spellbound by both the sacred and profane than ever before. Contact with the world at hand was lost or revived on an inscrutable schedule. So distressed was he by this condition, he had devised a plan for its rougher moments: If you get confused, sit down. If you sit down, stay put until the mind brightens.

He remained where he was, smoking Chesterfields with pointless determination, the ashes collecting in his lap. Picket lines formed in the underbrush beneath the skirt of trees. Then the guns played on him, and an ineffective hail of grapeshot bounced across the hood of the wagon. The Colonel withstood the onslaught, battling against the failure of the vision. Then came his capture and subsequent imprisonment at Fort Delaware, the parole, and at last the shameful journey home.

President Trass was a tolerant man, but eventually he became annoyed that his bird dog was baying itself hoarse.

WHERE PELHAM FELL

When Trass came out on the porch of the house he was born into, the Colonel noticed his advance and ducked down onto the car seat, felt immediately foolish in doing so, and rose back into view. He cranked open the window, shouting out with as much vigor as was left in his voice.

"I'm unarmed."

President Trass halted in front of the station wagon, wary of tricks. No telling what was up when a white man blockaded your drive. "Yeah?" he said suspiciously. "That's good news. What y'all want 'round here?"

The Colonel admitted his mission. "I'm looking for Kelly's Ford, where Pelham fell."

"That a fact," President Trass said. He slowly pointed in the direction the Colonel had come from. "You way off. You about two miles east of the crossing."

"Is that so," said the Colonel. "Much obliged." He stepped on the gas. A volley of mud kicked into the air over President Trass's head. The rear wheels spun in place.

Colonel Coates was invited into the house to wait for President Trass's neighbor to bring a tractor over for the car. They sat in the parlor, the Colonel on a threadbare sofa, President Trass in an overstuffed wingback chair. Neatly framed pictures were tacked in a well-sighted line across one wall: four tintypes of nineteenth-century Negroes; a sepia-toned group portrait with a Twenties look; an array of black-and-white snapshots, some of the subjects in the caps and gowns of graduation—presumably President Trass's ancestors and offspring.

To Colonel Coates's eye, President Trass looked like an old salamander in bib overalls, a slick, lymphatic edgelessness to the black man's features. President Trass thought that the Colonel, removed of the hat squashed onto his skull like a bottle cap, resembled a newly hatched chicken hawk, hot-skinned, old-ugly, and fierce at birth. They faced each other without exchanging a word. The longer President Trass considered the Colonel's *there*ness in the room, the more he began to believe that it was no coincidence, that something providential had happened, that Jesus had sent him a chicken hawk to relieve the Trass clan of the macabre burden they had accepted as their own for more than a hundred years, the remains of the soldiers President's granddaddy had plowed up on the first piece of land he cleared as a free man, a sharecropper in the year 1867. President Trass licked the dry swell of his lips, looked down at his own cracked hands as if they were a miracle he was beginning to understand.

"What you 'spect to see at ol' Kelly's Ford anyway? Ain't nuthin' there worth even a quick look."

"Eh?" said the Colonel.

"Say there ain't much there."

"That so."

President Trass kept his head bowed and prayed himself clean: Shared a lot of jokes, Jesus, me and You. First white man I ever *invite* through the door and You lettin' me think he some kinda damn cracker angel. Why's that, Lord? Well, I ain't afraid no more somebody goin' take this all wrong, leastwise this ol' chicken hawk.

"What's worth seein', I got," said President Trass.

The Colonel coughed abruptly and squinted. "I'm not the man who would know," he said.

"You come lookin' for soldiers, you must be the man. They's yo' boys, ain't they?" said President, and he led the Colonel out back to one of the cold sheds and gave him the bones that four generations of Trass family couldn't quite decide what to do with.

So the Colonel had defied Dippy, his wife, sneaked out onto the road ostensibly to buy dog food, and was returning home with two dirty burlap sacks full of what President Trass had described to him as noisy bones. Bones they were, laced with rotted scraps of wool and leather, too sacred for canine bellies, and tasteless anyway. But no noise to them the Colonel could detect, other than the dull rattle and chalky shift they made when he and the old black fellow carried them out of the shed and hoisted them into the rear of the station wagon. President Trass had what he and the Colonel agreed was accurately called a nigger notion: The bones talked too much, jabbered like drunk men in an overcrowded rowboat; the men whose flesh had once hung on these disjointed skeletons were still in them, like tone in a tuning fork, refusing the peace of afterlife in favor of their military quarrels. "That's a voo-doo I never had use for," the Colonel grumbled. "Men our age always finding queer ways to pass the time." "I ain't yo' age as yet," President answered back, "and I never said I had trouble fillin' a day like some folks I know."

Colonel Coates wasn't a man to heed mere telling, nor to concede to age what age had not yet earned or taken. "All right," he said to the black man. "With all respect for your habits, I am duty bound to recover the remains of these brave boys."

"That's right. Take 'em," President said. "You might just be gettin' some nigger notions yo'self. Prob'ly do you some good."

"I've been waiting half my life for a younger fellow to set me straight," the Colonel said, "and I don't reckon you're him."

"Well, Colonel," President Trass said with a tight smile, winking at the sacks of bones in the car. "You finally get in with the right crowd to tell you a thing or two."

Since turning eighty, Dippy Barrington Coates slept more during the day, catnaps on the sofa in the den, a quilt pulled over her legs, not because she was tired but because her dreams were more vivid and interesting than they had ever been before, and nothing she witnessed in them frightened her. She hadn't slept so much in daylight since 1942, when she was always tired. Awaking from those naps back then she had been miserable. The extreme loneliness of the dead seemed in her, as if she had been spinning in solitude through the blackness beyond the planets. That ended, though, when she left the house to become a nurse. After the war Taylor came home from Europe. It took some time for him to become her friend again, to settle in his own mind that he wasn't going anywhere without her the rest of his life. The migrations began again, so many places, so many homes she created only to dismantle them a year or two later.

But none of the early years were as hard to endure as the three before the last. Taylor, infirm but alert, first his prostate and then the shingles, which left extensive scars across his shoulders and chest, issuing orders from bed: I want this. I want that. Goddamn the pain, let it off for sixty blasted seconds. You're a nurse, do something. Dippy, have you fed the dogs? Has the *Post* been delivered yet? Did you hire a boy to pick the apples? Dippy, come up here and tell me what's happened to your ability to fix simple egg and toast.

The house and lands were too much for her to manage alone. She had secretly put herself and the Colonel on the waiting list at Vincent Hall up in Fairfax. There were days when she wished to God that He would make Taylor vanish into history, which was what the man had always wanted anyway. Just as she became acclimated to the regimen of his illness and moods, he popped out of bed one day fifteen months ago, announcing he would occupy his last days touring the fields of battle in the area. He recharged the battery in the Ford pickup and motored down the cedar-lined drive on his excursions, to be grounded semi-voluntarily three months later after what seemed like, but wasn't, a premeditated string of collisions, mad acts against authority. He plowed into a Prince George County sheriff's patrol car, a state-park maintenance vehicle, a welded pyramid of cannonballs at New Market. None of these accidents injured more than vanity and metal. Each occurred during a low-speed drift, the Colonel mesmerized by the oblique and mystical harmonies played for him by Fredericksburg, by Manassas, by New Market, where the cadets had fought.

She had made him sell the truck rather than repair it. Taylor sulked and groused for several weeks, the pace of his recuperation slackening to a plateau. He entered a year of book reading, map gazing, talking back to the anchormen on the television news, typing letters to the editors of papers in Washington, Richmond, and Charlottesville, disavowing the new conservatism because its steam was religious jumpabout, lacking in dignity and too hot-blooded for an Episcopalian whose virtue had never faltered to begin with. *Are we cowards?* one letter inquired about a terrorist attack on an embassy. *Many Americans today seem to think so. We are afraid we are, but I tell you we are not. What the true citizens and families of this nation have learned is not to abide by courage wasted.*

Writing in his study on the second story of the antebellum brick farmhouse, Taylor could look out across hayfields and orchards to the Blue Ridge. He found the gentility of the view profoundly satisfying. On stormy days the mountains were purple. Dramatic shafts of light would pierce the clouds, and the Colonel was reminded of the colors of the Passion and Golgotha. For his grandchildren he penned accounts of the clan, the Coateses and the Barringtons and Tylers and Holts and Hucksteps, hoping to seduce them into a fascination with their heritage, the precious ancestral silt deposited throughout the land. *My grandpa,* he wrote, *was Major Theodore Coates of the Army of Northern Virginia. He was assigned to General Early's staff and fought valiantly for the Confederate cause until the Battle of Antietam, where within an hour's carnage he was struck directly in the ear by a cleaner bullet. The wound itself was not fatal, but it destroyed the Major's inner ear, denying him his equilibrium and orientation and causing him to ride in front of his own artillery as they discharged a salvo over the lines. The charge lifted horse and rider far into the air, so witnesses said.*

When one of the grandchildren, a boy at college in New England, wrote back that the rebellion, not to mention the family's participation in it, was too disgraceful and produced in him a guilt by association, Taylor responded, *You might reasonably suppose that your forefathers were on the wrong side in this conflict, but I assure you they were not wrong-minded, no more so than the nation itself was. White men weren't slaughtering each other because of black men, that was clear from the start. Read about the City of New York during those years. When you go into Boston on your weekends, what is it that you see? Do you really mean to tell me that Northerners died to save the Negro from us?*

What do you think of communism? he had asked a married granddaughter last Christmas. It's foo-foo, she answered, and afterward the Colonel decided he had communicated enough with the newest generation. Altogether it was a serene year Dippy and Taylor had passed in each other's company, and neither of them had much desire to go beyond their own land. When once a week she took the station wagon into Culpeper to shop, Taylor would occasionally come along, and he did not protest being demoted to the status of a passenger.

She knew last night had been a restless one for him, though. Troubled by a vague insomnia, the Colonel had slipped out of bed three or four times to listen to the radio, stare out the window at the silhouettes of the outbuildings in the Appalachian moonshine. When he urinated he said he felt as though the wrong stuff was streaming out, not liquid waste but vital fluid. Nights such as this he felt were nothing more than waiting to kick off into eternity, to blink and gasp and be a corpse. At breakfast his shingles burned again and his breathing was more constricted. He had difficulty concentrating on the morning paper. He complained that his tongue seemed coated with an aftertaste of medicine that even her coffee couldn't penetrate.

After lunch Dippy snoozed on the couch, the afghan she was knitting bunched on her chest. When she awoke she went right to the kitchen door, knowing he was gone. It was wrong of Taylor to do this to her. Trusting him had never been much of an issue in the course of their marriage except when the children were growing up, and only then because he played too rough with them, wanted them to learn reckless skills, and showed no patience for the slow art of child rearing. He had once knocked out Grover when the boy was twelve years old, demonstrating how to defend yourself. Throughout his life the Colonel had been a good enough man to admit his shortcomings, by and by, but now he had survived even his ability to do that.

She walked nervously around the house, emptying the smelly nubs of tobacco he had crammed into ashtrays, thinking about what she might do. Nothing. Phone the sheriff and have the old mule arrested before he banged into someone and hurt them. That would serve him right and placate the annoyance she felt at Taylor's dwindling competence, three-quarters self-indulgence and willful whimsy anyway, she thought, the man trespassing everywhere, scattering his mind over too much ground. It was as though the Colonel had decided to refuse to pay attention. If he hadn't returned within the hour, she would call Taylor's nephew in Warrenton for advice. In the meantime she couldn't stay in the house alone, marking his absence.

She put on her black rubber boots, cotton work gloves from out of a kitchen drawer, a blue serge coat over her housedress, wrapped a red chiffon scarf around her tidy hair and knotted it under her chin. On her way out she turned the heat to low beneath the tea kettle. In the yard the dogs ran up to her and she shooed them away, afraid their clumsy affection would knock her down.

Behind the house the pasture was sprayed with wildflowers for the first time she could remember, the result of a Christmas gift called Meadow in a Can from one of the grandchildren. She walked out into it and the air smelled like sun-hot fresh linen. She went as far as the swale, sniffed at its cool stone dampness, and headed back, the dogs leaping in front of her, whirlybirds for tails. She went to the tool shed and found the rake and garden scissors, thinking she'd pull what remained of last autumn's leaves out of the ivy beds, and cut jonquils to take inside. Below the front veranda, where the boxwoods swelled with an aroma that Dippy associated with what was colonial and Southern, she tugged at the ivy with the tines of her rake, accomplishing little. Then the Colonel came home.

The station wagon bounced over the cattle bars sunk into the entrance of the drive and lurched ahead, slicing gravel. She looked back toward the road, wondering if Taylor was being chased, but certainly he wasn't. Dippy reached the turnaround as he pulled in, swerving and skidding, making white dust. One of the front fenders was puckered from the headlight to the wheel well. She stamped over and rapped with the handle of the rake on this new damage Taylor dared to bring home.

He remained in the car, veiled behind the glare on the windshield, his hands clawed to the steering wheel, reluctant to drop them shaking onto his lap while he suffered his pride. The dogs barked and hopped into the air outside his door as if they sprang off trampolines. Dippy kept rapping on the fender with the rake, harder and harder, drumming shame. His jaw slackened and his shoulders seemed no longer able to sustain the gravity of the world in its orbit. He prayed for composure, for the muscle of his reckless heart to beat furiously against their damn devilish luck, the fate that had made them two living fossils, clinging to the earth with no more strength than moths in a rising breeze.

The Colonel rolled down his window. "Stop that," he ordered.

"You are a hazard, old man."

"Stop that. I won't stand for this Baptist behavior."

"Come out of there."

"Here now, stop that and I will."

Well, Dippy did cease her banging on the fender, but she didn't know what to do next to emancipate the sickness that came when she realized Taylor had launched himself back onto the highways where he was likely to murder himself. She jabbed at the fender with the rake once more.

"What was so important you had to sneak off like a hoodlum?"

"Bones," he said too loudly, "bones," followed by a sigh. He had jumped ahead and had to backtrack his explanation.

"Dog food," he corrected himself. She knew better and he had to tell the truth. "I wanted to see where Major Pelham fell, that's all."

She wanted to cry at this irony—an old man's irrepressible desire to see where a young man had died—but she could only shake her head. Taylor coaxed his limbs out of the car and she listened skeptically to him tell the story of what he had been up to. "Noisy bones?" she repeated after him, becoming alarmed. This was not the sort of information she took lightly. He brushed past her to open the tailgate on the wagon. She frowned because inside she felt herself straining to hear the muddled end of an echo ringing across the boundlessness. Was a message being delivered here or not? Her longevity had made her comfortable with the patterns of coincidence and happenstance that life enjoyed stitching, cosmic embroidery on the simple cloth of flesh. She tried to make herself extrareceptive to this peculiar sensation of contrivance, but nothing came through.

"I think you've finally gone cuckoo, Taylor Coates," she said.

"None of that. These are heroes." He patted the sacks. "Gallant boys."

Dippy was bewildered. Goodness, she thought, what sort of intrusion is this? Who's to say how she knew, or what sense was to be made out of it? A bridge formed between somewhere and somewhere else, and Dippy understood that the man who had given the Colonel the bones was absolutely right—they were *noisy* bones, not the first she had met either. Oh, you could call those invisible designs by so many names: intuition, spirit, and ether, witchery and limbo. Don't think she didn't reflect endlessly about the meaning of each word that could be attached to the force of the unknown. Even as a child her life had been visited by startling moments of clairvoyance and fusion. Each instance felt as if she had just awakened at night to someone calling through a door.

"Look," the Colonel invited, and peeled back the lip of burlap to reveal the clean dome of a skull.

She had dreamed and redreamed such a thing. There were occasions in Dippy's life, each with its own pitch and resonance, chilling seconds when she attracted information from the atmosphere that translated into impulsive behavior: refusing to allow children out of the house, once persuading Taylor not to buy a horse because she sensed evil in the presence of the animal, sending money to a Buddhist temple she had entered briefly when they lived in Indonesia. She avoided riding in cars with Connecticut license plates if she could. As a nurse at Bethesda Naval Hospital during the war, she watched a sailor die on the operating table after hearing her son's voice say, *He's a goner, Ma.* What about you? she thought. You're dead too now, aren't you? And then she held her tears while still another dying patient was wheeled in.

There are a few things you don't know about me, she had said to the Colonel in February when he saw her mailing a letter to a scientist she had read about in the paper, a man at Duke University who researched these phenomena.

That's not right, he answered. After all this time.

Yes it is, she said. Secrets are what crones and children thrive on.

The Colonel pawed through the bones, exhibiting a look of sanctified pleasure. Warriors in a sack, seasoned messengers of glory. Conscripts from the republic of death. Dippy cursed them like any mother or wife. Dog food indeed. Why else were the bones here but to tantalize the Colonel with their chatter?

"I suppose we better call the police."

"The police!" the Colonel said. "Never. I'm going to find out where these poor boys belong."

"There's only one place bones belong," she said.

"They'll take their seat in history first," Taylor insisted, shuffling the bones he had pulled out back into their sacks. He straightened up, frail and indignant.

"God wants those souls placed to rest."

"No. He don't, Dippy. Not yet He don't. Not till I find out who they were."

Rally them, Colonel, rally the boys.

As Dippy expected he would, given his interests, the Colonel became obsessed with the bones, the necroscopic opportunities they presented, and she readjusted her daily life to accept the company of both the living and the dead. Because she had forbidden Taylor to bring the two burlap sacks inside the house, he spent his time in the workshop that adjoined the garage, paying little attention to much else than his mounds of dusty relics. Every two hours she brought the Colonel his medication. At noon she brought him lunch and tea, and at four o'clock each afternoon, for the full five days he spent in the workshop, she took him a shot of brandy to tire him out so he'd come willingly back to the house, complaining of the heaviness in his arms. Between trips to the workshop she'd fuss with needless cleaning, cook, or nap, instantly dreaming. She dreamed of her first daughter's elopement in 1939 with a German immigrant who later abandoned her. Once she dreamed of the good-looking doctor who plunged his hand into her drawers when she worked at Bethesda—she woke up smoothing her skirt, saying,

Whooh, that's enough of that. And she dreamed of the two of her children in their graves, a little girl from influenza, the boy who died during the liberation of France. They would stay in her mind all day after she dreamed them. Not so great a distance seemed to separate them now, and she took comfort in the sensation of a togetherness restored. Even a long life was daunted by its feeling of brevity and compression.

And Taylor out there in the garage, history's vulture, pecking through the artifacts. She dreamed him, too, atop a horse, leading his skeletons toward the fray into which they cheered. They cheered, and the extent of her sadness awakened her.

"How do we teach our souls to love death?" he asked her in bed the evening of the second day, the fumes of wintergreen ointment rising off his skin.

"Who says you have to bother," she said. "Leave those bones alone."

"They'll be placed with their own," he answered. "I'm working on it."

What do you remember of your life? the Colonel had asked President Trass in the shed. It ain't over yet, President said. But I remember everything—the gals, the dances, the weather. What about white men? the Colonel was eager to know. President answered, They was around. Then he told the Colonel about his nigger notion and said take the bones because there wasn't a Trass alive or dead who was willing to put them to rest. Not on Trass property anyway.

The Colonel cleared his worktable of underused tools and spread the contents of the sacks across the length of its gummy surface. He turned on the radio, lit a Chesterfield, and surveyed what he had. He counted twelve pelvic cradles but only ten skulls and nine jawbones. One of the jaws had gold fillings in several of the bare teeth, evidence attesting to the integrity of hate passing through generations of Trass caretakers.

Well, twelve men then, a squad, a lost patrol, eighteen complete though fractured legs between them sharing twenty feet, one still in its boot. The first and second day the Colonel reconstructed what he could of twenty-three hands from two hundred and sixteen finger joints. He divided the ribs up, thirteen to a soldier.

Something curious happened, but he didn't speak of it to Dippy. Metal objects in the workshop began to spark him, fluttering his heart when he touched them, so he put on sheepskin gloves and wore them whenever he was out there. His hands became inept and the pace of his work slowed. He started the third day aligning vertebrae into spines but gave it up by lunch. His interest transferred to those material objects that fell from the sacks: the boot with its rattle of tiny bones, a cartridge box with miniballs intact, a flattened canteen, six belt buckles (five stamped CSA), a coffee can he filled the first day with copper and fragile tin buttons, indeterminate fragments of leather, and scraps of delicate gray wool.

On the fourth day he brought to the workshop a wheelbarrow-load of books and reprinted documents from his study in the house, prepared to concentrate on the forensic clues that would send the boys home. The weather changed, bringing a frost, and his legs cramped violently. Dippy helped him carry a space heater up from the cellar to supplement the one already glowing in the shop. When she delivered his lunch on the fifth day, she found him on a stool bent over the table, his reading glasses off-balance on his nose, a book opened across his thighs, lost in abstraction as he regarded the buttons arranged in groups of threes. He appeared not to notice when she set down the tray. The radio was louder than usual. Easter was a week away and the announcer preached irritatingly about the sacrifices Christ had made. Dippy turned the sound off. Taylor looked up at her as if she had somehow thwarted his right to sovereignty.

"I'm close, damn it all," he said, scowling, and yet with a fatigued look, the remoteness quickly returning. "These are General Extra Billy Smith's Boys." His voice became unsure. "The Warren Blues, maybe."

"You don't have to tell me how close you are," she said. "I can hear the racket they're making."

The Colonel waved her away and she left. Dippy did not think his devotion to the bones morbid or absurd, only unnecessary, wasted time for a man with nothing more to spend. She could have told Taylor, if he believed in what could not be properly understood, the nature of the noise the bones were making. The bones were preparing to march. She loathed the clamor they made, a frightening, crazed exuberance. She returned to the house and suffered the grief of its emptiness.

That night a thunderstorm moved in from the west, blowing down the eastern slope of the mountains. The Colonel couldn't sleep. He stood at the bedroom window and peered out, seeing atomic sabers strike the land. He slid back under the covers with his wife and felt himself growing backward. His muscles surged, youth and confidence trembling once again in the tissue. Here too was Dippy, ripe in motherhood, squirting milk at his touch. And here were his school chums, the roster of names so familiar, Extra Billy's Boys one and all. *Company D. Company K.* Fellows he grew up with. Well I'll be, he said to himself in wonder. I went to school with them damn bones.

On the sixth day Dippy went to the workshop shortly after Taylor, disturbed by the extreme volume of the radio music coming across the drive. Pushing open the door she was assaulted by a duet from Handel's *Messiah,* the words and music distorted by loudness. The Colonel was on his feet, at attention, singing with abandon although his lyrics were out of sequence with the broadcast of the performance for Holy Week:

O death, where is thy sting? O grave, where is thy victory?

His face turned red and waxy as she watched in anguish. His shirttails flagged out between his sweater and belt, the laces of one shoe were untied. The Colonel seemed trapped between euphoria and turmoil, singing to his audience of skulls propped along the table. His voice became cracked and tormented as he repeated the lines, faster each time and with increasing passion. Dippy, thinking the Colonel had gone insane, was scared to death. She hurried to the radio and pulled its plug from the wall. Taylor gradually became aware that his wife had joined him. He felt a funny pressure throughout his body, funny because its effect was a joyous feeling of weightlessness—he could levitate if he chose to. He tried to smile lovingly but knew he failed in his expression. Dippy stared back at him, mournful, one hand to her mouth, as if he were a creature unfamiliar to her. Then a calmness came to him.

"Dippy," he bargained feebly. "I don't wish to be buried in my blue suit."

She helped him back into the house, insisted he take a sleeping pill, undressed his dissipating body, and put him to bed. She couldn't raise him for supper, nor did he stir when she herself retired later in the evening. She woke the following morning startled by the sound of the station wagon leaving the garage. By the time she reached the window, there was nothing to see. She telephoned the police to bring him back, covered herself with a house robe, and went to the kitchen to wait.

Two hours later the curator at the Warren Rifles Confederate Museum in Front Royal observed an old man enter the building and perform a stiff-legged inspection of the display cases. Afterward, the same old man approached the curator with a request to view the muster rolls of the 49th Regiment. There was nothing unusual about the old man's desire, and the curator agreed. He offered the gentleman a seat while he excused himself and went into the archives, but when he returned to the public area with the lists, the old man had left.

As he waited for the curator, the Colonel was overwhelmed by a sense of severe desolation. The room seemed all at once to be crowded beyond capacity. He felt claustrophobic and began to choke. The noise was deafening, unintelligible, and he was stunned to think how Dippy and President Trass could tolerate it.

In the car again he felt better, yet when the road ascended out of the valley to crest the Blue Ridge, suddenly the Colonel couldn't breathe the air for all the souls that thickened it. He died at the wheel, his hands grasping toward his heart, the station wagon sailing off the road into a meadow bright with black-eyed Susans, crashing just enough for Dippy to justify a closed coffin. The undertaker was a childhood friend of Taylor's, loyal to the military caste and the dignity of Southern families, understanding the privacy they required when burying their own. With discretion he gave her the large coffin she asked for, assisted her in carrying the two heavy satchels into the mourning parlor, and then left, closing the doors behind him without so much as a glance over his shoulder to witness her final act as a wife, the act of sealing the Colonel's coffin after she had heaped the bones in there with him.

She was dry-eyed and efficient throughout the service and burial in the Coates's family plot outside Warrenton. Children and grandchildren worried that she was holding up too well, that she had separated from the reality of the event, that when the impact arrived she would die too. She could have told them not to concern themselves. She could have told them how relieved she was to be the last Southern woman, the last of the last to lower the men who had broken from the Union into their graves, how relieved she was to hear the Colonel exhorting the bones, *Keep in ranks, boys, be brave,* until the terrible cheering grew more and more distant and their voices diminished and she was finally alone, free of glory.

I ATE HER HEART

It was a wretched act of love and greed. I was in Galveston, playing the mouth harp with the Stank Brothers Band and crewing on the shrimp boats when they wanted me. She was another woman from Dallas who figured she'd look hurtfully sweet and sexy with the Gulf of Mexico as a backdrop. My Starlene, she was right. I fell for her hard. There was a miserable turn of circumstances. I made an irresponsible decision and took a bite from her heart. It was a sour thing.

Lord, how I suffer the loss of her. My Starlene was an inspiration to me. She smelled like a lime tree and had legs like a movie star. I never had it so good.

We met at the Wildcatters Picnic, where the Stank Brothers were providing the noise. Me and the brothers noticed her right off down in front of the stage. It looked like she was reading our message loud and clear. Playing in a band you get used to a lot of girls being friendly. When the music picks up speed, they start behaving like they got lightning in their pants. She was parading herself in green terrycloth short-shorts tugged right up into her Alabama, and a tube top of similar color wrapped tight around her bosom. Her legs were so long it looked like it would take all day to run your tongue down them from hipbone to heel. After a few songs this old boy came up to dance with Starlene. He was swinging and dipping her. They were moving fast to the rag. I thought, My God, those boobs are going to pop and sure enough one did. Without breaking step she tucked it back in like I might do my shirttail. I remember nodding to Roy Stank and saying, That's a fine woman there. I remember him nodding back and smiling like a weasel.

She settled in my mind right then. I thought of her as I played. My music started coming through in a purer form than it ever had before. I blew the Texas dust through those reeds. I sucked in the frontier and the longhorn steers and the Alamo. I spoke a version of Spanish and Apache and rattlesnake. I courted my mother's mother, charmed from her her toughness and suspicion. I took all the bums of the range up the tracks to Kansas City and back. My lips were burnt and bleeding by the time I finished.

She found me over by the van liquoring up between sets. I like my liquor, God knows I do, and that's a part of this story. I've always handled it well, but when you start chasing grief with booze you're in for a second world of trouble all your own.

Well, she comes up to me. The Brothers were inside the van, and they began to caw and squeal when they saw her. The Stanks knew no restraint. They're in the back of the van hitting up methiolade and sniffing canisters of Freon they tore off old refrigerators. I saw in her eyes that this woman had some tenderness to her, so I said, Let's you and me take a walk, thinking I'd never have a chance with her if she got in the van. She did poke her head through the door and say, Boys, you make it all worthwhile. They grabbed for her but she declined their invitation with a wise little laugh. I put my bottle-free arm around her high waist and we promenaded through the parking lot.

She said, "Mouth man, you've got a talent that makes me wonder what you're truly like. You've got a style."

I appreciate words like that, and I told her so.

"You're a good-looking man too, a good-looking ugly man."

"I know how you mean," I said. It took a long time for my ugliness to smooth out into something beneficial.

"They're the best," she said. "They don't suffer without good cause."

I knew what she meant. She was talking to the history of my heart.

She stopped by a willow tree, told her name, and pressed against me. I put my face into the curve of her neck. Her skin smelled like lime, a sweet, fresh, citrus sting. My nose is a weak part of me. More than once it has led me into love. I could feel it happening again.

"Mouth man," she whispered in my ear, "I'll bet you know how to treat a woman fine."

I let my hand crawl up her back and explore her curly hair. She lifted one of her long legs and hooked it behind me. We kissed and rubbed together. "I do," I said. "I do."

Starlene expected a lot out of those words, and I'll be damned if I didn't give it. Knowing what fame was for, I took her home with me that night and bedded her. In the morning fame went right out the window, and love swept in like new air filling a dead space. We spent the day licking on each other. By the time the sun went down, and I fixed her coffee, I wasn't the Mouth Man anymore, I was just me, Parris Deaks.

You know the course of such passion. She moved into my place, came with a suitcase full of pretty clothes, a big box of shoes, a transistor radio, and a bag full of stuff that filled every spare inch in the bathroom. She cleaned things up, though in a disregardful way, and put a picture of her daddy on the shelf next to the bed. None of that bothered me. My life had taken a step up. I was grandly in love. I had been in love with women before, but I couldn't recall when or where or who or how. Starlene seemed like the one and only. Women have always been important to me. I need to treat them like queens, but I never had one before who knew what she needed from me. Starlene needed the queen treatment, and I gave it to her.

At dinner I'd cut her steak up into little pieces to save her the trouble. When she took a bath, I'd scrape her skin soft and pink with one of those Japanese sponges. She'd get her monthlies, and I'd go into labor pains out of sympathy. She'd sneeze like a little kitten, and I'd get on the phone to the doctor.

The way I felt, I couldn't do enough for Starlene. I'd smell her smell, or ponder those legs, and get in a helpless state of giving. Her fondness for cocaine, I'll say, was not to be denied, and I did my best to accommodate her with what little money I had. She'd dope up a lot, but I never said anything. It seemed to bring her so much pleasure. She didn't usually get far off like some dopers do. As I said, I go for the booze, so I'd just sit beside her and drink until she fell into my arms. We'd drag into bed, undressing as we went. She'd turn on my unit and stick in a tape, always the Bonecrushers or Nellie Slit. She'd take the headphones and put them on. I'd nuzzle down between her thighs and have my ears clamped by her burning flesh. Locked in like that, I'd play her night lips in a harmonic fashion. She'd shove into me as if she wanted to be swallowed up. Occasionally I'd look and see the ecstasy of her face on the horizon.

Do you get what I'm saying here? I was in love. I was way down in love and never wanted to come out. It was the best thing that ever happened to me, and the worst.

After a couple of months she said to me, "Trailers ain't a decent place for life to advance."

I hadn't thought about it before. "Right," I said. "What did you have in mind, honey? One of those condo things? A cabin in the woods?"

"I like the water," she says. "I like the smell of it and the way the sun moves around like mercury on the surface."

I searched about and found an old houseboat docked at a marina in Trinity Bay. The guy wouldn't rent it but said he'd sell cheap. I was cash poor, so I called up my shrimper friends Jim and Joe (not their real names). They were organizing a run to Mexico and took me along as a favor. Everything but shrimp ended up on that trawler. My cut was large enough to buy the houseboat and something special for Starlene.

When I came back eight days later, she wouldn't go with me to the band jobs anymore. "Why'd you have to be away so long?" she said. "The Brothers sound like birdshit without you, Parris."

I held her in my arms and told her how much I missed her.

"I hate being alone," she said, looking at me straight. "You were always in my heart, Parris." She let go of me and placed my hand over her left breast. "Right in here, kicking like a baby. I never forgot about you for a second."

I said I wouldn't leave her again. I gave her the ghetto blaster I had bought her for a thousand bucks—a high-technology unit that sent out enough sound to kill everything in a forest or sustain life in the barrios. My hands trembled when I gave it to her. She said, Oh my, oh my, and cried.

"No one, Parris," she said, "not ever, has been this nice to me. I've always felt like property in a war zone, seized and abandoned, over and over."

"Aw hell, Starlene," I said, petting her hair.

"I suppose it's my fault. I need a lot of love and attention. Love me, Parris. Pack my heart full."

I told her I would.

"Forgive me my sins," she added.

I told her she was without sin in my eyes, that the devil wouldn't dare come near a soul like hers.

I leased this rundown dock in a secluded part of the bay for our houseboat. We seemed alone together in the world. I could piss off the side in the daylight if I wanted. She could sunbathe bare-assed, expose her real estate to the wild blue yonder. With a fishing pole or crab net, she'd snare creatures from the deep and transform them into spicy gumbo. The best thing for Starlene was when our house rocked cradle-like in the wake of a passing motorboat. It got to the point where she craved that rocking more than anything.

One night she said to me desperately, "Oh dammit, Parris. I don't think I can sleep with everything so still. Even these quaaludes won't take me out."

We made love, but still she kept her edge.

"Maybe it's the coke making me so restless," she moaned.

I'll see what I can do, I told her. There wasn't much I could do. I tried holding on to the dock and jumping up and down, but the hull had too much concrete in it to move that easily. The next day I drove over to the wharves, where an old buddy of mine worked on the supply end of a drilling team. He sold me a crate of dynamite at a pirate's price. After that I'd blow a stick in the water whenever Starlene had trouble sleeping. We'd get about a fifteen-minute roll out of it, and if she wasn't out by then, I'd blow another. I never heard a complaint from anybody on the bay except once from a rich lady about the dead fish in the water. I said it was my intention to eat those fish, and it was no business of hers.

Sometimes we'd sit out on the deck at night slapping mosquitoes and stargazing. We'd count UFOs. The sky always seemed full of them. If the mood was right, I'd spit some blues through my harmonica. She'd hum a lazy counterpoint that would amuse me. I forget how long we had been on the boat by then, but it was during a peaceful night like this that I asked her a question that she'd been avoiding.

"Starlene," I said. "Nobody has a thirst for music more than you. When you going to come with me to another job? We're booked at Gilmore's Friday night."

The way she said *Never* made we wonder what was on her mind. Then she recovered. Her face came out of a shadow into the light of a candle that burned between us. I could tell by the set of her eyebrows that she was ready for finding fault in the world. "You ask that awful Roy Stank for a raise. Do that, Parris," she said.

I was low on cash again, had been thinking out loud that very day on what chance I had to get on a shrimper. I knew Starlene had a good point. But I wasn't deaf to the basic revelation of her words. "What's wrong with Roy?" I asked. "You've not said bad about him before."

"Never you mind."

"What in the dickens does that mean?" I said. It was the only time I raised my voice to the woman. "Roy do something to you while I was away? He make a move?"

"No such thing," she insisted, clipping her voice. "It's

you he's doing something to, Parris. Roy ain't giving you what's due."

I said, "Now honey, that's Roy's band. I don't play on every song. I don't have loans out on fancy equipment. I may be the best harp man in the South, but what's fair is fair."

"We need more money," she tells me.

"Cocaine ain't salt," I said. "You have to slow down."

She changed tack on me. "Parris," she said tenderly, "I can't have you going off on those boats. I was never meant to be alone."

"Neither was I."

"Then stay," she said, moving toward me for an embrace. "Roy will give you more money. That band pulls in a lot. Where would they be without the weight you add to their sound?"

"The question is, where would I be?" I told her. We didn't talk about it again that night.

About a week later, when we drove home from dinner at the Evil Enchilada, I noticed that the old boat had suffered damage—she was down a foot in the water. I got a bilge pump going, but the best I could do was stabilize the situation. Starlene was crying, and I hated to see that. Whenever she slipped into tears it made me feel like a dog.

"Must've been the dynamite," I said sadly. "The shock waves must've cracked the cement of the hull."

"Aw Parris," she bawled. "I loved our home. I love the creak and the sway."

"Don't you worry, baby," I said. "We'll have her hauled out and patched. You'll see."

"Homeless again," she sighed.

"Now don't worry," I told her. "We'll stay in the van until the work's done."

We rolled up our pants to keep dry and went below to

I ATE HER HEART

collect our clothes. She spent some time in the bathroom doing something to improve her mood. When she came out she was smiling what I'd call indiscreetly. Thinking back, I'd say she was calculating how to survive the narcotic hunger she lived with.

"We can stay with Roy," she said. "He'll put us up."

I didn't think that was a good idea. Roy wasn't much of a man without a guitar in front of him, and Starlene herself had applied the word *awful* to the fellow. The van would have been fine with me, but I went along with the scheme because I wanted her to have what she wanted, no questions asked.

We got over to Roy's place around midnight. The Brothers were just waking up. The house, a stuccoed old-style thing with red tiles on the roof, stubby palm trees and motorcycles in the yard, used to be nice but the boys had turned it into a pigpen. Between the needles and the dogs, the wall-to-wall shag was unkind to bare feet. One of the band's fans had taken a blow torch and written FUCK YOU and ROCK OFF in fire all over the walls. Two stereos were going at the same time, playing different numbers at top volume. Living with Starlene, I had become accustomed to a certain level of cleanliness. The Stank place was reprehensible. I thought maybe I could take it for a day or two. I suppose you have to live hard to sing right.

The Brothers were gathered in the kitchen for what they called their breakfast. There was no table, but they stood around eating vitamin pills. They had no other form of nourishment that I ever saw besides Buckhorn beer and orders of ribs from Smiling Goofus McTeez, that barbecue place run by some old black guy gone crazy on his Scottish ancestry.

Anyway, Roy was combing the knots out of his hair

with his fingers. He looked unrested for just getting out of bed.

"Roy," I said. "Bad luck's come upon Starlene and me."

He became very concerned. He wanted to help us, he said, in any way he could. I was a brother, he said. Starlene asked for a vitamin. Donnie threw some capsules in her mouth. I took a beer from the fridge but had to wipe brown sludge from the top of the can before I could drink it. One of Roy's hounds ran through the room so fast he skittered all over the linoleum, then crashed out a small hole in the back screen door. We made powerful music together, but I sure didn't like socializing with the Stanks. Their habits were lethal. They had minds like a trash dump on fire.

I opened a second beer. There was some disjointed small talk that came right from outer space. Everybody's eyes seemed connected to a rheostat—they just kept getting brighter and brighter. Starlene's too. She said, Oh dear, this is *good*, and giggled. The Brothers grinned like jackasses. Buzz found a ukulele in one of the cupboards and started strumming out this calypso shit. I was bored, tired, and uncomfortable.

I said, "Starlene, let's go lie down and nap."

She looked at me like I was spoiling her party. Her pupils had dilated fully, her flashing green eyes eclipsed by dark moons. Her face explored a series of expressions until it found something right, something serious and deliberate.

"Ask Roy now," she said.

"Ask him what?"

"Ask me what?" Roy joined in.

"You know," she said to me. She was by my side now, holding my arm with both hands. "Ask him."

"Ask me what?"

I ATE HER HEART

"Starlene," I said gently. "This isn't the right time. We're here enjoying this man's hospitality." What the hell was she doing? Maybe she wanted to be sure I wouldn't leave her alone again, but the way she kept going, I had to think it was deeper than that.

"Ask me what?" Roy persisted.

"A matter of business, Roy. Nothing much at all. We'll talk about it another time."

"Go ahead. Ask me."

"Naw, Roy. Some other time."

"Go ahead, brother."

Starlene took over, or we might have gone on like that all night. Her voice was squeaky and vicious. "Roy," she said. "You're going to have to pay Parris more money, or he'll have to leave the band."

"Well, honey, come on now," I said, like it was a joke. "That's not true."

Roy was rather delighted by Starlene's proclamation. "Is that right?" he said, looking at her, not me.

I tried to intervene. The two were making a kind of connection I couldn't break. "Roy, forget what she said. Donnie, what'd you give her?"

"Is that right?" Roy repeated.

"Yeah," she said. "You know it."

Roy howled and clapped his hands, a gesture that made me think he was a maniac. "Well, how 'bout that," he said. He was just tickled pink. "Donnie!" he yelled without ever turning away from Starlene, "how 'bout that?"

"Shame on you, Mister Deaks," Donnie said.

"Buzz, how 'bout that? What do you think?"

Buzz pouted his lips. "This ole boy is pussywhipped."

"How 'bout that? Lester, you have some thoughts on this?" Lester didn't. He had laid down on the floor with his eyes closed. He was in poor condition for talking.

Starlene was smoldering, and she broke out in flame. "Roy Stank, you are a worm," she hissed.

"But you like that, don't you, gal?" he said. He smiled wickedly and finally dropped his stare. He turned to me instead. "This little bitch has got you fooled, Deaks."

"Roy, don't say such a thing," I told him.

"This girl likes to gallop up the side of heaven and shout at the angels. Starlene's in love with the snowman, Parris. Ask her what she was up to when you was out on the Gulf."

I don't like fighting, but I was ready to strike the man. Starlene commenced to tug me out of the room. "We can't stay here," she said. She said it over and over again until we were at the door. I heard the Stanks back in the kitchen laughing ungallantly. "My honorary Brother," I heard Roy shout after me. "Just say the word and I'll take her off your hands."

"Come back anytime, Star Queen," one of the other Stanks called out. "You know how generous the Brothers can be."

Starlene ran across the driveway ahead of me, shaking her head and screaming, *Damn, damn, damn*. When I caught up with her, she spun around. "Hit me, Parris," she said. "Go ahead."

I'd never do that.

"I fucked up," she said. "I did you harm. You must hate me."

I held her, cuddled her head to my chest, smelling that scent of fresh lime behind her ears and along the tense curve of her neck. "You did no harm," I told her. "You own my heart. That devil tried to twist his way in, but it didn't work."

"Jesus God, don't ever leave me, Parris."

"I'd never do that," I said.

We had the houseboat hauled out of the bay and put in

dry dock. I parked the van next to it, and we quartered there. I said no more to Starlene about what happened because I knew no good would come from talking of it. For me the glory of the Stank Brothers Band was no more—I had to seek other employment. I went to see Ed Chiles of the Kamikaze Kowboys. He said the Kowboys were going into the studio in another month or two to cut their next album, and they could use me then. I did some roustabout work in the oil fields for about a week. The boatyard finished repairing the houseboat and handed me a hell of a bill. The yard wouldn't release the boat, though, until I paid in full. Starlene had no patience for anything. One day she took a job as a waitress at a nice seafood restaurant nearby but quit before her shift was over. She stayed in the van more and more, nodding to the tape deck, then at night when I was there she'd whine and complain. The tan on her legs began to pale. It didn't prejudice my love for her. I only became more determined to set our world back in balance.

To be precise, it wasn't more than eight or nine days like that until Jim and Joe (not their real names) showed up in the yard the same time I was arriving from work. They talked a lot of vagueness and indirection, as all of these fellows do, but from what I gathered they were doing something big and needed me along to replace a member of the crew who had misbehaved publicly and gotten thrown in jail. On an operation like this sums of money are not clearly discussed beforehand, but I was made to know that I would earn enough money to buy a new dick if I wanted one after the run was over. I discussed it with Starlene. She said no, she wouldn't be alone again. I said to her, Honey, this is the windfall we need to live a life free and unmolested. She sulked all night but finally gave in. I left before noon that next day.

Being with Jim and Joe can get dangerous because they don't give a shit what they do. Smuggling wetbacks, guns, heroin, pot—it's all the same to them.

This particular run was a junket for six Mexican thugs who couldn't afford the formality of airports and borders. We picked them up in Cancún, off the Yucatán. They gave Jim a garbage bag full of money for their passage.

I watched them come aboard at night. I know a little Spanish, so I asked them who they were.

"Nosotros somos Los Huevos Grandes," they said audaciously, as if I was breathing air only because they allowed it.

I thought that *huevo* meant egg, but I didn't laugh. People from other countries just don't think the way we Americans do.

These greaseballs were well-heeled. They all wore silk shirts of the most terrible colors. Their underarms smelled like overcooked chili. Two of them had briefcases handcuffed to their hairy wrists, and each of them wore more jewelry than I've ever seen on any woman except a back-alley whore. They were going to Galveston to deposit money in special bank accounts, get checked out at the gringo VD clinics, visit the cathouses they owned in the barrios, break the arms of the upstarts that were trying to move in on their action.

These Huevos liked to touch their knives and shout at each other. I tried to keep away from them as much as I could, but they were bad headlines from the word go.

Halfway through our cruise the passengers were having trouble relating to each other. A boat's not a place for people with no tolerance. Toward the end of the voyage I was fool enough to try to break up a fight between two assholes in the galley. The one they called Aguila took more than his share of rice and beans at lunchtime. One of his buddies stabbed him in the hand. I stepped in, and immediately there was a switchblade pressed across my throat. Another guy came up and wanted to slice off one of my ears to teach me the big lesson—don't interfere in the business of Los Huevos Grandes. He was laughing and thought it would be a great prank. Jim walked on the scene just in time. He told the Huevos that if any of them fucked with the crew, they could tear up their round-trip tickets. That message twice saved my life.

Bad weather drove us in near Port Lavaca, which is by car not more than three hours south of Galveston. The Gulf is big, the Coast Guard small—you're always banking on luck in a deal like this. We snuck into the inter-coastal waters and anchored in a tiny hideaway cove in Tres Palacios. On shore you could see the sandy tracks of a fisherman's road winding through the dunes down to the water.

After we set anchor, Joe tuned in the short wave and contacted one of his local men for some transportation. The plan was for me to escort the passengers to a roadside motel, check them in, and pay for the rooms. Then they were on their own to get to Galveston any way they could to rendezvous with the ship in about ten days. I could do whatever I wanted until it was time to head south again. In the meantime, Jim and Joe would enter the harbor to wait for better weather and then move the shrimper up to home port.

Joe gave me fifteen one-hundred-dollar bills. I was to pass a thousand of that to the wheels man, pay for the motel, and keep the rest for pocket money. I ferried the Mexicans ashore and told them to lay low in the dunes until the transportation arrived. Rain kept falling the whole time. I longed for Starlene. I wanted that lime smell to open my nostrils. I wanted those sleek legs wrapped somewhere around me.

Jim came along the last trip and returned the Zodiac to the boat. From shore I watched the props churn up mud as they reversed out of the cove. I was alone with the six goons and didn't much care for it. I was also dying for a drink, a little taste to relax with. Nobody had much to say to me. I tried to be as polite as I could because I knew damn well there wasn't five seconds worth of trust among us. Paranoia isn't something that bothers me much, but this group wasn't exactly the Jaycees. I knew I had to be careful.

Los Huevos passed reefer back and forth and talked in shrill, bitch-like voices. Then one of them, Aguila again, the fellow with the appetite, found a sea turtle. It was a female. She had recently crawled up on the beach, probably thinking it was a quiet enough spot to scoop a hole for her young. They chopped her open and ate the eggs. When they were through, they stood around telling one another how virile they would all now be. I thought to myself, These savages make the Stank Brothers look like young Republicans.

What there was of the sun was fading into general bleakness by the time the transportation arrived. A big International Harvester all-purpose vehicle, its side and back windows blacked out, came roaring across the sand flats to where we were in the dunes. We packed in and got the hell out of there.

"Jim says there's a motel you know of that guarantees privacy," I said to the driver. He nodded once, kept his eyes straight ahead. We bumped and banged our way out to a surfaced road that led to Point Comfort.

I ATE HER HEART

"When you see a liquor store, stop," I said. "I got to buy a bottle or I'll go crazy. These egg fellows are bad on my nerves." He offered me some reefer but I passed it up. That stuff makes me sleepy and loosens my overall confidence. I had a night ahead of me and needed to be in control.

We stopped at a small bait and lure shop with a package store attached. I bought a fifth of whiskey. The Mexicans bought a couple cases of good Scotch, a case of Winstons, and a box of beef jerky. I was impressed by the quality and quantity of their thirst.

At the motel we came to everybody waited in the vehicle while the driver went inside. I considered going with him but then thought better of it. I looked like a tramp, unshaven, clothes dirty and wet, smelling like diesel fuel. I cracked my bottle and drank from it like it only held water.

The driver reappeared. "Gimme four hundred bucks," he said. I did. He left and came back within a minute, handing me a single room key.

"What's this?" I asked.

"Waz thees?" one the Huevos echoed, his voice full of hostility. I had the sense this guy wanted to start a war.

"That's all the man had. Be thankful for it, buddy."

"This is bad," I said. "These boys are already claustrophobic from the boat."

"Keep a low profile now," the wheels man said as he returned to his seat. "Don't bother other guests. Everybody's got to be out of there in three days."

I paid him off and escorted the passengers across a dark patio to the room. They griped a lot among themselves about being forced into one room, but they didn't pester me with it. As soon as we got in there they began to fight over who was going to use the bathroom first, who was first on the phone, who would get to sleep on the twin beds. I told them not to be so loud. They told me something that I believe meant fuck off and die. I began to worry that being with them was becoming bad for my health.

Bring us food, one of them told me.

"All right," I said. "What do you want?"

They wanted Kentucky Fried Chicken. A lot of it.

"Right. Try to hold it down while I'm gone," I warned them quietly. Like I said, I was just trying to be a nice guy, do my job, and get back to Starlene, as quick as I could and in one piece.

The motel was on the edge of a commercial strip. Once I was outside, I placed a long-distance call to Starlene from a booth across the street. I phoned the boatyard and had somebody go get her on the line. Her voice sounded very weary when she asked me where I was.

"Starlene," I said. "I'm with a bunch of people I don't like. Come rescue me."

I gave her directions and hung up. It was about eight o'clock. I walked down the road a ways and bought three buckets of chicken and a tub of coleslaw. By the time I got back to the room, the Mexicans had dug into the booze and were celebrating their safe arrival in Los Estados Unidos. They wolfed down the chicken and slaw and were soon noisy again. I tried my best to pacify them, but it was useless. Each of them had his own bottle of Scotch. A few of the guys were tying off their veins and shooting up. Somebody came toward me with a hypo, but I waved him away. He threw the thing at me as if it were a dart. I dodged, and the needle stuck in the lampshade behind me. He laughed, and I joined in nervously to let him know I could take a joke. If I had any sense I would have gotten out of there, but I figured I was safe, that business is business, and Jim had warned them not to harm me.

I lay on one of the beds drinking heavily from my bottle,

I ATE HER HEART

my nerves all jangled, wondering if I should stay in the room until Starlene showed. By ten o'clock I had finished my fifth but didn't feel the way I wanted. I started in on some of the Mexs' Scotch. The head honcho, who still had a briefcase locked to his wrist, kept dialing the phone, making contact with his people in Galveston.

This gang liked a fast track. They didn't impress me as being a tightly run organization, though. You can never trust low-life to stick together, even if they are goddamned eggs, or Big Balls, or whatever the hell Huevos Grandes is supposed to mean. I had not before been with men of such petty and brutal character. One of the junked-out boys accidentally burned Aguila with his cigarette. A knife was drawn and brandished. He was talked out of using it, but everybody wanted to yell about the incident. From what I could tell, they were trying to convince each other they were the nastiest lot of people on the planet. Aguila was an exceptionally swarthy man, a guy with droopy ears and nose and a mustache that looked as if it were coated with shoe polish, who usually hung back from everything. But whenever he joined the action, it was like throwing nitrate into a toilet bowl.

I didn't want a part of what was going on, but I didn't know what else I could do. I was drinking away my discomfort, pining for Starlene.

Eleven-thirty.

Twelve o'clock. She loomed in my mind like a big wave about to crash down. She wasn't there yet. I stared at the door as if it were my future, trying to understand what went wrong. Whenever I looked around at Los Huevos, all my eyes could see was blood lust.

By one o'clock I was itching I needed her so bad. Then I heard the knock that would provide my salvation. The fiesta shut down in an instant. The Huevos hopped up, dug out their guns and knives. The atmosphere was suddenly pure poison.

"It's all right," I said with confidence. "That's a friend of mine."

She came through the door. Roy was with her. They were both going a thousand miles an hour.

"Roy, you skunk," I recall saying. "What the hell you doing with Starlene?" I looked at Starlene for an answer, but there wasn't much to see on her face. She was on the moon.

"She wanted company, man," Roy said. He was dirtier than me and without good reason. He had an outlaw face, stained mustache, bad teeth, patched blue jeans, odoriferous T-shirt. I hated everything about him now, even his long beautiful fingers that could play a guitar so fine.

"Don't say another word, Roy," I said. "I'm in a dark mood." I gave him a hundred-dollar bill for fare back to Galveston and started to throw him out the door. He didn't resist. Roy had a big build and a lot of meanness deep in him, but I wasn't afraid. One of the Huevos moved up behind me. I looked at him and realized he was going to jump on Roy if Roy remained in the room another second.

"It's all right, it's all right," I said. "No problem. Just a friend who's leaving." I guess the Mexican considered Roy's presence a threat to their operation, especially after they saw how I behaved toward him.

Just as I had Roy outside, he squealed, "Starlene's gonna sing with the Brothers. Fuck you, Deaks." I knocked him in the side of the head with my fist and slammed the door on him. Starlene had been absorbed into the midst of the Mexicans. I forgot about Roy and went after her, grabbed her cold hand roughly.

"Is that true, honey?" I asked, tears forming in my eyes. The booze had gotten me into a terrible state of release.

"What?" she said thickly. "Oh."

"You singing with the band now?"

"I am?" she asked. She was all confused. No telling what Roy had gotten into her.

My heart was pumping strong for her. She was dressed in a dainty peach-colored sundress. Her curly hair frizzed out from under a sharp-looking straw Panama. I wanted to be alone with her and cuddle, drop Roy from my mind. One of the Huevos grabbed her ass. I pushed him gently away. My adrenaline couldn't find its way through all the alcohol in my blood.

"None of that," I said. "Time to go. I'll see you boys in Galveston."

We reached the door right as Roy was coming back through it, talking a supersonic line of apology and regret. If he had had the time, I think his intent was to beg a ride with us back to Galveston, seeing as how Point Comfort is at the back edge of nowhere, but the world jerked ahead to his speed before he had the chance to make amends. Los Huevos came in on us before I knew what was happening. Roy fell dead or dying into the room, his neck opened by Mexican steel. A grinning Huevo swung his knife at me but then restrained himself, allowing the blade to penetrate my chest only superficially right above my heart.

He immediately threw his hands up in innocence. "Meestake, beeg meestake," he said, still grinning like he had only stepped on my toe. He pointed at the door and said, "Gal-vees-ton."

I looked at the Huevos standing over Roy. Strange, but only Aguila hadn't been in on it. I stood up straight, feeling no pain, and went for the phone. Somebody put his hand on my shoulder, and Starlene began to scream.

"No policia," the Huevo with his hand on me said. It was the same guy who had just cut me.

"Right," I answered him. "No policia. Just an ambulance, that's all." I dialed the operator.

The Mexican took the receiver away from me, yanking the cord from the wall outlet. Starlene was still screaming. I turned in time to see Aguila lurch out of his corner. He was smiling wickedly. He wrapped a fat hand around Starlene's pretty lips, and they commenced to wrestle. I was a step apart from them but never made the distance. I felt no pain, only the blow from behind and my nose squashing as I hit the carpet.

This is the trouble that can visit a peaceful man sometimes.

The place was silent when I came to. The Huevos had cleared out of there. It seemed like I should have been dead, but I wasn't. Starlene was stretched out on the bed like a forsaken angel, her peach dress ragged up and blood-soaked, a tired smile locked on her bruised mouth. I bolted the door and went to her.

"Don't look at me so cold, Starlene," I said. "You know how sensitive a man I am."

I lay down next to her on the bed. I kissed her, squeezed her. There was no smell of sweet lime on her like there always was before. It wasn't good, she wasn't for it anymore. She was gone.

That fact grieved me deeply. I let her rise up to heaven on my grief. As I pressed her against me, my left hand caught in a hole just below her armpit. I pulled my fingers out of the chilly flesh and looked at them, then at her. She was slashed everywhere, as if the Huevos all needed to get inside her at the same time. Knife language—this was the only tongue the Huevos spoke fluently.

I reeled up from the bed and started drinking the liquor left in the room until I was as crazed as a man could get. Then I lay back down next to my love. I wept without

I ATE HER HEART

shame. I cried, Don't leave me, baby. I lost consciousness. When I woke up, it must have been hours later. The room was shadowy and smelled foul. I wept again. I cried, If you go, Starlene, you take too much of me with you. I gave you more than I knew I had.

The drunkenness had left me, but I had fallen into a delirious condition. There was a large pain in my chest, and I imagined it was the loss of Starlene's love. This was how it felt when two hearts were separated forever. I knew that if there was any love left, it would have to be located in her. That's where I would find it and restore myself.

I settled down and considered these thoughts. She had a long cut right below her breastbone. I stuck my hand in there and wiggled it up under the ribcage until I gripped her heart muscle. I just held it, waiting for something to run back into my veins. I fell asleep that way. The rest might be a dream for all I knew. When I withdrew my hand, I thought I had found what I was hoping for. In my palm was a hard little pearl. I studied it and thought, This is me, this is my part, what I gave her, the seed that got inside like a grain of sand in an oyster and grew to be love. I bit into it, believing that I had to get it back circulating in my own flesh. I spit it out, it was such a sour thing. The agony in my chest remained unsoothed.

This is all I'm going to say about it. It's been bad enough already. I spent three days alone with her and my wretchedness until they busted the door down and dragged me out.

They tagged me for conspiracy to aid and abet the illegal entry of aliens. The cannibalism charge that was finally dropped got a lot of attention from the press. I had to take the heat for Jim and Joe, although Los Huevos now conduct their business from behind bars.

My lawyer was expensive and encouraged the judge to

show compassion in the end. I'm not in prison or the nuthouse but spending six months on a model farm with a high reform rate.

Oh Starlene, I miss you sorrowfully.

Not too long ago this tweedy fellow drops by asking me if I've changed. Yes sir, I have, I answered him. I'll never do a foolish thing like that again, I swear. Do you regret your deeds? he asked. Mister, I don't, I said. Except in a legal way. He left and I went back to watching the soaps on TV.

I stay up all night thinking things over. I'm not a bad man. I didn't hurt anybody, no one died by my hand. I guess I've been around the wrong sort of people too long. Somebody's been a poor influence on me. Maybe it was just her, the way she made you believe you were giving so much, and it was paying off, like you were making smart investment uptown. Isn't there a Mexican saying that goes something like, You eat the heart, or the heart eats you? Maybe I was thinking of that when I ate the damn thing.

I think somewhere there's a woman who'll understand what I did, the right and the wrong of it, and come to comfort me.

Honey, get in touch. I'm ready for love again.

I ATE HER HEART

CELEBRATIONS OF THE NEW WORLD

It is July Fourth and my mother-in-law has decided that since Lorraine and I were married in a courthouse without family present, now is the time for the two households that are joined in us to come together. I am not happy with the idea, especially since my own mother has turned that basic, intimate idea into an extravaganza.

We will meet at my wife's parents' house in the Chestnut Hill district of Philadelphia. My side comes east a week early to sightsee in Washington. They drive in for the occasion from Moberly, Missouri, and thereabouts in two station wagons, a Monte Carlo, my father's kelly-green Cadillac, and rented Winnebago—except for Uncle Alabard, who flies into Dulles Airport from the West Coast the day before the reunion.

My parents stay with me and Lorraine and the baby in our town house near the Torpedo Factory in old Alexandria. The rest of the folks, the aunts and uncles and cousins, the nieces and nephews and grandchildren, stay at the

Marriott Inn in Rosslyn. They linger at breakfast each morning, enchanted with the view of the city from the rooftop restaurant. I am there also, their tour guide, waiting to herd them across the river and march them along the streets of the capital.

Together my relatives represent a substantially homogenized group. They are clean and slow, responsible and readily impressed. My father became rich during World War II mining fire-brick clay from the rolling, unimaginative landscape of central Missouri. Only when he first started the business did he really have to labor at it. Afterward he took life easy, fishing and hunting, raising bird dogs, and watching my mother, the perfect small-town matron, organize charity fund-raisers at the Moberly fire station. He would send her off on days-long shopping sprees in St. Louis, Kansas City, or Chicago, and he took these opportunities to drive down the road to Columbia to attend the basketball games and to flirt harmlessly with the girls at the university.

As for the rest of them, I can't remember exactly who does what. My uncles (except for Alabard) and cousins are, I believe, farmers, and I suspect my father has bankrolled each and every one of them as restitution for not allowing my mother's side of the family into his business. I am grateful to my father for having had the imagination not to farm. It's no secret that I have never appreciated my Midwestern heritage. As I grew older, the dusty streets of Moberly seemed like bars across my life. I felt like an eagle stuffed into a shoe box, a symphony played on a Jew's harp. I am still sensitive about it, but that seems to be gradually passing now that I am relocated and independent, have a family of my own, and look forward to making a name for myself in the maze of corridors on Capitol Hill.

The kids all want to stay in town for the Fourth to pack in one more visit to the new Air and Space Museum and to hang around until dark when the fireworks go off at the Washington Monument. I align myself with the kids, but it's the matriarchs who have the final say, as they always seem to do when family business is at stake. My mother thinks it's a grand idea, an *inspiration,* to wrap up their trip with a dinner and celebration in the City of Brotherly Love—the sponsor of the Constitutional Conventions and home of her favorite forefather (you know who, and she never misses an opportunity to quote him saving pennies). Although Lorraine's mother, Rose, has organized this, and although she really had something smaller in mind when she talked to Gloria, my mother, on the phone in December, she has accepted Gloria's single-minded vision and even joined in the spirit by inviting her husband Bernie's cousins from New York City and sending Uncle Joachim Elrojo (Bernie's last living brother) a round-trip ticket to fly up from Mexico City. Rose herself is an only child—her parents died in a car accident in the Fifties—so she stands alone against the onslaught, especially since Bernie has started to slip away from her.

Lorraine and I make it a point to be the first to arrive in Philadelphia to help Rose with the preparations. Uncle Alabard, my father's only brother, wants to ride up with us. I haven't seen him since I was a boy, but I know that he usually lives in Las Vegas, taking his chances with the money he earned originally by investing in Dad's mines thirty-five years ago. In the car, Albie (he asks us to call him that) amuses the baby with coin tricks and celebrity imitations. His Peter Lorre is pretty good; his Jerry Lewis, appropriately clumsy. Lorraine and I both fall in love with the guy. At the tollbooths on the turnpike, Albie rolls down his backseat window and tries to talk the attendants into flipping a silver dollar for double or nothing.

"Where I come from, see," he says in the voice of Jimmy Cagney, "anything goes."

We reach the Schuykill Expressway by noon. A yellowish dome of humidity and pollution presses down into the city. Albie talks about staying an extra day, renting a car, and driving over to Atlantic City to see some fellows he knows who have maneuvered casino gambling onto the ballot in November. What a dream, to get in on the ground floor of that one, Albie tells us. I turn away from the downtown area and count the stoplights to Jefferson Boulevard.

I pull into the Alazars' long driveway. We are relieved by the coolness of the shady oaks and maples and evergreens. The smell of boxwoods is colonial and delicious. The flagstone house stands up out of a girdle of ancient azaleas and rhododendron. Double chimneys rise above the steep black-slate roof at both ends of the house. It was built in 1821 by Rose's great-great-grandfather, who fled his native Cork County in Ireland, accused of the murder of a queen's magistrate. Rose insists that the man was guilty only of patriotism.

I park and walk around the car, and Lorraine hands the baby out to me so she can get out. Lorraine is her usual bright, dynamic self. She gets frantic, and she gets meekly depressed, but I have never seen her sour. Since she cut her black hair boyishly short at the beginning of the summer, her dark, moist eyes (like her father's) dominate her face, foreign and penetratingly mystic.

Rose's two poodles are out on the lawn. They run up yapping and sprinkle my sandaled feet with excited drops of pee. Albie mistakes them for ankle biters and is reluctant to leave the car. Curiously, it is Bernie, not Rose, who answers the doorbell. Lorraine and I are fully aware of

Bernie's condition; for the past year now, Rose has found something to occupy him when she expects visitors. Bernie's face is set, as if he's waiting for us to come to the point. A white frost has settled deeper into his hair since we saw him several months ago.

"Rose," he calls back into the house, "the pizzas are here. How much is it?" he says, fishing into the pockets of his baggy trousers.

"Hello, Daddy," says Lorraine, stepping forward to hug him. "How are you feeling?"

Bernie looks quite fresh, quite alive, deceivingly healthy. "Hello," he answers, looking at us closely, polite and then puzzled. I realize that he still doesn't recognize us, that he is foraging in the expanding wilderness of his brain, cast out from those friendly habitual places that made the world fit tightly together, and there is no spark of cognizance, no electricity flushing across the terrible dark gaps. When his expression turns to desperation, I imagine that while his heart pushes toward us he is furiously searching the margins of his mind for a note of information, an imperishable root, to verify his weak sense of knowing us. Rose's voice calls to us from somewhere in the house.

"Is that you, kids? You're early. Come back to the kitchen. If Bernie's there, bring him with you."

I throw my free arm around Bernie's shoulder and pat his back, guiding him along. We no longer seem a mystery to him. He bends toward the baby in my other arm, inspecting her, his face awkward. He pats her silky head softly, lovingly.

"Do you know who I am?" Bernie asks the baby. "I'm your grandfather."

Behind us Lorraine sighs with relief. She teasingly says, "Don't forget your daughter, Bernie. It takes one of those to make grandchildren, you know."

"Oh, yes," says Bernie without looking around.

We find Rose busy at the stove. All of the gas burners blaze with blue flames; a light on the microwave oven blinks on and off like a warning signal on a rough highway. Lids clatter against pots overboiling with steam and the rich, exotic aromas of cumin and garlic, olive oil and lemon. Rose wears an ironed flower-print apron over her brown cotton slacks and white sleeveless blouse. She looks harried but beautiful. Besides her daughter, she is the most energetic, capable woman I know. Because she chose to have a small family, she was able to have a career of her own, away from the house, away from Bernie. Now she's a special assistant to the president of Temple University, a job she loves. I can see her at the conference table, her elegant hands folded atop a black binder of statistics, her reddish hair igniting the hearts of her male colleagues.

Unlike Lorraine, however, Rose often gets carried away with her sense of duty. Lorraine has told me stories of Rose beating her on the head with an espadrille for the usual childhood offenses. I suppose that was the hot blood of her ancestors pulsing to the surface. I like Rose, though; she has always treated me like one of her own, but she has a way of assuming you agree with her, and forcing it when you don't. She is generous enough to ask my opinion (Gloria won't ask), but like my own mother's, her mind is always predisposed toward the rigid or the unpredictable.

Rose sets down her big wooden spoon to kiss us and hold the baby while I introduce her to my uncle. She is eagerly affectionate toward Lorraine, taking her daughter's hand in hers and not letting go, interested in how things have been for us. Bernie and Albie are looking at each other as if they don't know what to do.

"Bernie, this is Albie," I say. "Albie, Bernie."

"Alazar," says Bernie.

"Yeah?" says Albie. "I met this guy once at the Stardust who called himself Sheik Alacazar. Money was like sand in the desert to him. Couldn't play cards, though."

"Bernie's Lebanese. His father was ambassador to Washington after World War One," I tell him. "Bernie used to teach foreign affairs at Columbia."

"No kidding?" says Albie. "Say, you like to play cards?" he asks, pulling a fresh deck from the inside pocket of his pastel sports jacket.

"Sure," says Bernie.

The two of them sit down across from each other at the kitchen table. Bernie appreciates my uncle's card-shuffling ability. His eyes become the eyes of a priest fingering through a racy magazine, trying to concentrate and be casual and indifferent simultaneously. Albie smacks and pops the cards and they dive together like trained fish. Rose puts the baby into our portable crib and takes Lorraine by the arm. The two of them disappear into the expanse of the house.

"What'll it be, Bern?" asks Albie.

"Blackjack?"

The cards fly forward and I am at the liquor cabinet fixing myself a rum and tonic when the baby starts to cry. "She's hungry," Lorraine yells from the back of the house. "Her formula is in the blue bag."

I liberate a burner on the stove to warm the bottle. While I am waiting, I inspect the food that Rose is preparing. She fancies herself a superior cook of Middle Eastern cuisine (Bernie's magnanimity has encouraged this). She has created her specialties for our get-together. I wonder about this choice since the members of my family are corn-fed people and not generally adventurous or curious about what they put in their mouths. I sample the kibbeh

95

and pine nuts—overspiced and mediocre. The grape leaves are pasty inside.

Bernie ignores his cards momentarily to pick up the baby. She stops crying. He sits back down with her in his lap, propped up straight against his chest.

"Hit us," he tells Albie. Albie lays a nine on Bernie's king.

"Bust," says Albie.

Bernie slowly draws his down card toward him and shows it to the baby. The kid instinctively grabs it. Bernie carefully unwraps her fingers and tosses the card face up on the table. It is a two of diamonds.

"Twenty-twenty-twenty-one," says Bernie. He smiles bashfully.

The bottle is ready and Bernie insists on feeding the baby while she sits with him. I watch for any signs of trouble, but he remains attentive to both her and the cards. His dusky, Eastern eyes are serene. His freshly shaven jaw relaxes. I open cold bottles of White Horse ale for the two men and fix myself another drink. As a team, Bernie and the baby play against Uncle Albie. It is a rare, beautiful picture, something to hold on to, to preserve against the days ahead. I decide to go to the car for my camera and photograph the three of them together.

On the way back to the kitchen, I look through the bay window at the rear of the long living room and see the screened shadows of my wife and mother-in-law sitting in deck chairs on the porch. Beyond the house, the grounds are lush and thickly green, overcome with trees and filled with flower gardens. The strong, natural peace of what I see disturbs me in a way I do not fully understand. Perhaps it's only knowing that on the far side of the barrier of woods, less than a mile away, an urban nightmare, a monster of trash and neon and stone, is winding up for a holiday spree, and all leaves of absence on the Philly P.D. and Fire Department have been canceled. I return to the kitchen wondering what the two women are talking about.

"Your father-in-law is beating the pants off me," Albie says.

"Thatta boy, Bernie," I say. The baby has fallen asleep on his lap and he has set her bottle next to his own on the table. I take a light reading and snap away. Bernie starts talking in what sounds like German.

"*Der spichken vonbringst mein stubberflappen,*" he says. "*Lipshitz.*" He goes on and on.

"You go to school in Germany or something?" Albie asks him.

Bernie does not stop to answer. His magnetic eyes jump from Albie to the cards to me, confident that we understand what he says.

"*Ott blashauden meister,*" Bernie says. Suddenly he is quiet, his teeth clenched, the lines on his forehead pinched in confusion. "I don't know what that means," he says. But then he smiles cheerily.

Albie looks at me to confirm his guess that Bernie is playing a joke. I am laughing, and now Bernie is laughing with me, and I can only shrug my shoulders.

"He's getting old," I say.

"Geez, he don't look any older than me," says Albie.

"I have a disease," Bernie says indifferently. "Alzheimer's disease."

"No kidding." Albie doesn't know what else to say.

"Bernie's all right," I tell him. "In fact, he's in good shape. They fear this man out on the golf course."

"That's right," says Bernie.

"Sometimes he just forgets things," I say.

"You want to deal?" Albie asks, his one sure gesture of compassion.

Bernie deals. Rose bursts into the kitchen, with Lorraine several steps behind her. Their presence creates an ambiguous tension. I try to look at Lorraine, but she seems to be staring into space.

"Oh my God, look at the time!" Rose shrieks. It is one P.M. "Uncle Joachim's flight arrives in twenty minutes. You'll have to pick him up for me, Jack."

"That's no problem."

Lorraine says she will stay behind to help with the cooking and to greet the relatives when they arrive. She looks as if she needs to get out of the house, but there's no sense asking her to come along. Because Rose has never met Joachim, I ask Bernie what he looks like.

"He's red," says Bernie. He will say no more on the subject; his meaning is indecipherable. Rose adds what little she can.

"He's four years older than Bernie. In the Thirties he left Paris, where he was studying something peculiar—maybe it was linguistics—and followed Trotsky to Mexico. He even changed his name from Alazar to Elrojo. From the letters that he writes Bernie, he seems to be a very dedicated man. Nobody in the family has seen him since 1938, when he spent a year in Pittsburgh organizing the steelworkers. Just keep an eye out for a little old Lebanese-Mexican man with more nose than a face deserves."

Under a daisy pushpin, she finds the flight number on her bulletin board and gives it to me. Lorraine follows me out to the car. Her skin glows in the dappled watery light soaking through the trees. Her eyes are red. I can see she's been crying.

"Rose says Daddy's much worse," Lorraine tells me.

"You could see it when he answered the door. He didn't even know us."

"In the kitchen he was talking like a German, making the words up. Uncle Albie finally began to answer him. You would have thought they were at a beer hall in Dusseldorf playing pinochle."

Lorraine laughs and tries to hold on to her lightheartedness. She usually can and she does again. Her long fingers pick at the buttons on her blouse.

"Oh brother, Jack, what am I supposed to do? He's loony. My distinguished poppa's becoming a loony bird. Rose says that she always has to keep an eye on him now. Last week he was supposed to play in a tournament at the club and he put his golf bag in the car and drove around and around while his partners waited all morning for him to show. The first thing he asked Rose when he got home that night was, what were his golf clubs doing in the backseat?"

She pauses to emphasize what she is going to say. "A *policeman* had to bring him home. He couldn't find the street by himself. This from a man who has influenced American foreign policy. He'll put on his coat and start out the door without any idea where he's going. Rose had a special lock installed on the front door to keep him in. She lets him out in the back and he digs around all day like a mole and cuts flowers to bring to her."

"I should leave now or I'm not going to make it," I say.

"You've got to talk to Rose when you come back," Lorraine says. "Mom says that as long as he knows her she won't let him down, but I think she can't take it anymore and that means she'll commit him. She's searching for an answer, Jack. She feels so guilty."

I reassure Lorraine that I will talk with Rose, although if there is any decision to be made, I'm sure she has already beaten us to it. As I pull out, a black Continental with New York license plates squeals into the driveway. Its radio blasts out the Yankees game. Bernie's cousins from Queens, undoubtedly. They are very, very swarthy-looking, dangerous in my suburban imagination.

The holiday traffic around the city is heavy. I arrive at the airport late, my shirt drenched in sweat, but the flight is delayed. I wait in the bar, distracted, my thoughts occupied with those portions of Bernie's cerebrum shrinking like old grapefruit. I made a pilgrimage to the hospital on a Sunday afternoon in November with Rose and Lorraine and Bernie, an unpleasant family outing that ended in passing around a sequence of Bernie's CAT scans as if they were album snapshots. His brain appeared in the negatives as large cross sections of cumulus cloud rising out of celluloid, each of us marveling not at the growth of, say, a niece or nephew, but at the implosion and irreversible retreat of Bernie's moribund gray matter, crumbs of it plaqued and fallen in like sinkholes in a Missouri pasture.

About a month ago Rose wrote us that the doctors believed Bernie was approaching a crisis stage, a fork in the road where he would either become docile ("exquisitely passive" were the doctors' words—"Sure, as exquisite as a goddamn turnip!" Lorraine snapped when she read that) or quickly degenerate into unmanageable paranoia.

Now that we have seen Bernie, I know what direction his chemistry has taken (for how long, nobody dares to say), and that the country of his soul remains green and unviolated. There is still room for a man to live there.

I make my own sense out of Rose's determination to unveil Bernie, bring him out of the closet to parade clownlike before my embarrassed kin. In the past, she has outmaneuvered plans to bring us together as we are today.

Bernie was always out on the golf course with some statesman from Washington, or recovering in bed from the flu (she even made a point of saying *Russian* flu, hinting at some greater intrigue), or deer hunting in the Poconos. Rose now must have encountered her own Rubicon. Bernie's growing need for attention surpasses what she can give, threatening her job, which I know excites and fulfills her in a way that being a mother again does not. The dinner is a scheme to establish her pride and save her own life as her husband drifts away from his. Perhaps it is admirable and brave and honest. I think she wants to impress upon everyone what a banana Bernie has become. I think she wants to win our sympathy and then give him up as I suppose she must. And she wants Lorraine and me to say, Yes, Rose, you're doing the right thing.

Uncle Joachim's plane arrives. It is painted a tropical, ridiculous yellow. Through the waiting-room window I watch the passengers disembark. I am unable to spot any likely candidates to be Uncle Joachim Elrojo. Then, after the plane seems emptied, two stewardesses appear at the top of the mobile stairs. Between them the women are holding a very thin, very happy Kriss Kringle outfitted in a perfectly tailored white linen suit, a black string tie flopping below his neckline. Even from a distance I see that the man looks much like Bernie, and as the trio comes closer I can see the wrinkles on Uncle Joachim's face spread out from his eyes like feathers in a wing.

The stewardesses seem distraught and anxious, and seek relief from their charge. Uncle Joachim leans forward in their arms at a precarious angle as they descend the steps off the ramp. As they come through the gate, the flight attendants carry Joachim along with them; he's lifted right off the ground, still at an angle, and his feet seem to float up behind him. I am the only one left waiting there, and the stews bring him right to me.

"Hello," I say. "Was it a good trip?"

"If he's yours, sir," one of them says, "please, please take him. This old man has a nasty mouth."

"Not only that," says the other. "He thinks he's here for a revolution."

I marvel at Uncle Joachim's hair. It's as though someone has glued white fluffy goose down around his ears, under his nose, along his cheeks and chin. The aquiline nose on such a face cuts the air aggressively, and he stretches forward in the women's arms like a rooster ready to strike.

"Uncle Joachim?" I ask.

"Joachim Elrojo ha llegado," he says. *"No tenga cuidado."*

"Quite the contrary," the stewardess on his left tells me. "You've got a lot to worry about."

I don't understand Spanish, so I don't know what she is referring to. Joachim's voice is gentle, the tone as soothing as a hymn. The stewardesses release their hold on my uncle-in-law and he glides into my arms. We hug one another: I have embraced a soft plant, a fern, but his cheek is like the floor of the desert sanding my face. I look into his strong eyes as we pull away from each other and they sparkle with tears.

"Don't let him fool you," the stewardess says. I am beginning to dislike her unforgiving attitude. "He speaks English as well as you or me, and he's bilingually abusive."

"Trilingually," says the other. "You forgot what he said in Italian."

Looking at Joachim's unculpable, if not sleepy, smile, I cannot believe their accusations. He hooks his weightless arm around mine and we take slow, short steps toward the baggage area. He does not respond when I ask for a description of his luggage, so we wait silently among the animated crowd until there are no more people, and no more bags riding the circular conveyor belt. Uncle Joachim is untroubled by this mystery. I escort him to the claims office, where the old Trotskyite still refuses to speak, but the agent checks his manifest and announces that Mr. Elrojo had no luggage on the flight. Christ, I think, Uncle Joachim is quite a prankster.

Walking out through the main terminal, Joachim stops in front of the dark entrance to the cocktail lounge. He backsteps around until he has changed our direction and we are both facing it. The name FLYING HIGH pokes out of the painted clouds above the glass door.

"Let me buy you a cool one," he whispers.

I am delighted that Uncle Joachim has decided to speak to me, and in English, but I tell him we are running late, that traffic is bad, and the collective family awaits our arrival. Still, we drift into the lounge. Uncle Joachim is, I feel, and has been, in perfect inscrutable control of the situation. We advance to the bar and he asks for two ice cubes placed in two paper cups. He must repeat the request several times before the bartender can hear his light, accented voice. Joachim keeps one of the cups, gives me the other, and we leave.

In the car, Joachim digs behind him and pulls a silver flask from his hip pocket. I can see engraved on its front a falcon gripping a hammer and sickle in its talons, a serpent squirming in its beak. He tells me the flask was a gift from Trotsky.

"We were brothers," Joachim says. "I was speaking at a *campesinos'* meeting in Merida the day Stalin's dog tore him apart with an ice ax." He unscrews the cap and pours a clear liquid into my cup. It melts the remainder of my ice cube.

"Here," he says. "Just a taste for the road. Leon loved his vodka. Cheers. *Salud. Skoal. Prosit. Aloha. Pax vobiscum.* Here's to absent friends."

He downs his; I test mine, resting the cup between my legs. I pay the lot attendant and pull out into the fast lane. While we stood at the baggage area, I had explained to Uncle Joachim who I was, but he had not been interested. He did not know me, nor did he care. It was enough for him that I was there, that we had found each other, and that whatever it was we were doing was going smoothly. He had, I guess, long ago accustomed himself to nameless contacts, and esoteric arrangements that need not be mentioned twice.

Now he gazes straight ahead through the windshield at the cityscape smoldering in front of us. "Do you know," he says. "Do you know?" But I don't know if I do or not because he forgets me. I don't understand why the stewardesses were so critical of him. To me he is an old, leathery seraph, a veteran of tireless campaigns whose vision has trimmed all superfluous fat from body and mind.

I turn on the car radio, but Uncle Joachim immediately flicks it off and startles me by breaking into song:

> *"King Borria Bungalee Boo*
> *Was a man-eating African swell . . ."*

He switches to verses from *The Mikado* and I realize he is singing Gilbert and Sullivan songs I have not heard since I was in grade school. His voice is clear and firm, though a bit off pitch. He swings his arms up on each chorus and looks over at me as if he expects me to join in. After ten minutes, his enthusiasm falters.

"Those fellows," he says. "Bourgeois as hell, but they made people happy." He spends the remainder of the trip with his hands close to his eyes, inspecting the fingernails.

CELEBRATIONS OF THE NEW WORLD

Despite all the distance between them, I begin to see that Joachim Elrojo is truly Bernie's brother. He is another jewel in the family *fleur de lis,* a prophet called away from the bedside of Utopia. And, like Bernie, he seems to be a step or two beyond the rest of us.

The roads are jammed and by the time we turn into the Alazars' driveway it is late afternoon. Two entire teams of uncles and cousins and nephews play whiffle ball on the shadowy front lawn. They are all dressed in Bermuda shorts and madras seersucker short-sleeved shirts. White gym socks and black oxfords protect their feet from the zoysia. The women sit on lawn chairs in a sunny spot, gossiping or thumbing through sections of the *Inquirer.* My little nieces torture the poodles with affection, tying red, white, and blue ribbons to the dogs' collars.

Bernie's New York Lebanese cousins are nearby, spread out on military blankets, looking very much like gangsters and opium smugglers. As we come to a stop, they line up in a stiff row in front of us, heavyset and wordless, their wraparound sunglasses very threatening. My father has his movie camera whirring in his hand and films us getting out of the car. I keep a nervous eye on the Lebanese.

"Comrades," Joachim proclaims. He strides forward, a *comandante,* and gives each of his silent recruits a pat on the shoulder, a kiss on each cheek. They seem satisfied with this and march back to their blankets. I wonder what's going on; they are Joachim's cousins too, but I doubt if he's ever met them before. Joachim waves my father away.

"Por favor, no cameras," he says.

"You don't understand—" my father begins, but Joachim turns his back, beckons to me, and jerks his thumb at my dad. I guess Joachim wants me to throw him out.

"He's official," I explain. "He's one of ours."

"Okay," says Joachim. "But tell him to film from behind. Only from behind."

Rose steps out the huge front door of the house with a tray of bottled beer in her hands; Bernie is right behind her, and Gloria follows them both with a pitcher of iced tea and a pack of star-spangled Dixie cups. Bernie has not noticed our arrival. He remains in Rose's shadow while she delivers the beer to the ballplayers. When she finishes, she sets down the tray, takes Bernie by the hand, and leads him to us. She stops him in front of his brother, and the three of us—Rose, my father, and I—wait with anticipation. Joachim looks him over.

"He'll do," says *el comandante.*

Bernie's attention ascends through the trees, over the gardens, across our smiling faces, and alights on the Winnebago in the driveway.

"Say, whose is that?" he asks, taking a step toward it. "What do you call that thing?" Rose pulls him back.

"Bernie, look at this man. He's come a long way to see you."

Bernie looks right at Joachim without seeing. Then, degree by degree, Bernie falls into himself.

"It's Yusef, my brother Yusef!"

Uncle Joachim, too, finally comprehends the exact nature of this, his latest, expedition. Emotion bruises his eyes and spreads tears across his face in the many channels of his creased brown skin. The moment has such impact that my father lowers his camera in respect. The two brothers embrace and kiss each other again and again. Bernie is so much larger than Joachim and he holds his elder brother's delicate head to his shoulder. Sobs squeeze up out of Joachim's withered throat, an anthem to Alazar history.

"It's okay," Bernie tells him. "It's okay. It's okay."

Forgetting our presence, they release each other but

continue holding hands like two schoolboys. Joachim keeps his free hand over his eyes, and I wonder if behind the callused palm he sees the years that were never theirs together, and the early years long ago that were. They walk across the side lawn toward a bed of flowering peonies. Bernie sits on the grass and pulls Joachim down next to him like a lover. We can still hear him consoling Joachim. Rose observes them for several minutes and then turns to me. Her eyelids flutter spasmodically over her green eyes, little electrical twitches.

"Jack," she says. "I've got to talk to you." There is anguish in her face, or rather her mouth, which is pale and tight.

"I think I'll go see what Albie's up to," my father says.

"No, please stay," Rose tells him. "I need you to hear me too."

My father acquiesces; he chooses to bow his head so that his presence is minimal. I already know what Rose will say, and because she is going to say it, I feel genuine— what?—not love, but genuine *something* for her. Perhaps it is love, and I worry that I will become emotional.

"Jack," she says to me, "what should I do?"

Of course, I tell her that she must think for and of herself. But I doubt the credibility of my own advice. I try to read my own heart—I don't know what I feel. Or what I should say, how I should act. Maybe I'm afraid, but then what's to be afraid of?

"Yes," she says. "You're right. But it's so hard to do that after thinking of everybody else all this time. At least I hope I was thinking of them and not just myself."

I nod my head to comfort her.

"And I have to tell you," she says, "if you don't know already—it may be hereditary. From what I've seen of Joachim, I'd say it was."

107

"I know," I say. "And Lorraine knows too. We've seen the statistics."

Rose looks at my father to check his reaction to the news, for this thing in the Alazar blood has swum generations to find his grandchild. My father raises his head to meet her troubled eyes. Never have I seen his face so benign and glistening, so overtaken by the anima. This is a part of my father that has been denied me.

"I reckon they're like two kids," my father says, "dressed up like old men." He reflects on this in his slow, Midwestern way, which so many of his business competitors have misjudged in the past. Averting his eyes, he says, "This is a nice way for a man to close up shop. There are not many fine endings left. Who dies happy these days?"

Without knowing the full story, my father seems a little envious of Bernie and Joachim. I see no sense in outlining for him the terminal features of this dry-brain disease. They are no blessing. I suppose he imagines they will be spared the sharp peak of lucidity that perhaps washes through the soul before the knock and entrance of death. My father will not. He has survived one heart attack and lives in fear of the second.

"But it's wearing me down," says Rose. "I'm getting tired."

"I understand," my father says: the voice of a minister about to fly up to heaven.

"I know when I'm unhappy," she says. "Some people don't. They just let themselves be mean."

"Hire a nurse," I say. My innocuous suggestion pierces the air around us and there is a moment of brittle, conspiratorial silence. I realize suddenly that through Rose I am rehearsing my own future with Lorraine.

"Believe me," she says slowly. "I've thought and thought about that. I just can't keep watching him."

"The nurse will watch him."

"No," she says. "I mean before my eyes. I can't take Bernie losing his mind right before my eyes. I can't watch *it*."

"I understand," my father says.

"I better see how Lorraine is doing in the kitchen," she sniffs. In a minute she calls from the doorstep that dinner is ready.

My father rounds up the sweaty ballplayers, the gabby aunts, the chubby nieces. He understands, and I suppose I do, and Lorraine does, but my mother, I know, will not. She will pounce on Bernie's illness like a small girl rescuing a bird with a broken wing. She believes that people are unloaded into rest homes the minute their hearing goes bad or are hidden in institutions the second time they misplace their car keys. This represents a great un-American crime to her. No family, I have heard her insist, can ever divide itself if its members truly love one another, which they should if they're related. Common blood is like Super Glue to Gloria. I have also heard her say she doesn't worry about old age because she knows her children will take care of her as she once did them. She's wrong.

I collect Bernie and Joachim from the peony garden. Bernie's eyes are bulging forward into the diminishing sunlight like ripe olives, and phlegm speckles his bright lips. Apparently a word has stuck at the back of his mouth. His effort to overcome the dysnomia sends only preverbal vowel sounds sliding carelessly off his uncooperative tongue. He has never appeared more witless to me. Joachim reminisces about their boyhood together in the District of Columbia, frequently interchanging Bernie's name with Leon's. His use of the present tense makes me instinctively look ahead of him into the clouds of flowers to see what he sees there.

"We take the streetcar out to Hains Point," Joachim

says, "to line fish for bass and scoop out the herring with our nets when they're running. You are afraid of the water and afraid of the colored people. When we get home Poppa says to you, 'What did you catch, Leon? What fish is that I smell?' "

"It's okay," Bernie finally says. He can say whatever he wants as long as it isn't *Help*.

"Time to eat," I tell them.

I stand them up and brush the pink petals off their pants from the blooms they have unconsciously picked apart while talking. We are the last ones into the house. The downstairs bathroom has been invaded by relatives crowding the marble-topped sink. The upstairs bath presents too much of a challenge for my slow-moving companions. I take them to the kitchen sink and turn the water on for them to clean up. Lorraine is there, spooning food into silver chafing dishes raised above disks of transparent flame. The bowls look sacrificial, antediluvian; they glimmer with ceremonial potency.

Uncle Albie is uncorking brown bottles of wine. Rose removes a large crock of chilled cucumber soup from the refrigerator. Joachim cups his hands under the faucet and splashes the cool water onto his face. Bernie thinks this is a good idea and does the same. Lorraine stands by, shyly waiting to meet her uncle, but the two brothers are still throwing water around.

"*Ver gut,*" says Bernie.

"*Que bueno! Que delicioso!*" Joachim declares. By the time he turns around, the shoulders of his suit are soaked gray and his hair has turned to paste.

"Uncle Joachim," Lorraine says, taking off her apron, drying his face and then Bernie's. "I'm Bernie's daughter Lorraine. Ever since I was a little girl I've been romanticizing about you."

Out from under the apron, Joachim's head looks wrapped in cirrus, his fine, tousled hair wisping over the topography of his features. He takes her hands and brushes his lips against them in a gesture of Old World graciousness.

"Bernie," he says. "Bernie, you never told me you had a daughter. She looks just like Teresa." (None of us know who Teresa is. And Joachim has been told of Lorraine through the mail.)

"I have two daughters," Bernie says, and he looks around the room for the other one. Almost three years ago, the other one, Sherry, dropped out of graduate school and joined a group of Gurdjieff cultists in Oregon. Nobody in the family hears from her anymore.

We all move out of the kitchen toward the dining room. Lorraine and I take baby steps to accommodate Bernie and Joachim. The doctors refer to this in their more affected moments as *marche à petit pas*. The maple table has been pulled apart and four leaves added to its middle. It now extends from the rock fireplace at one end of the room to the French doors that frame the sunset at the other. The golden rays flash off the silver and china and crystal arranged on the table. Everything looks very proper, very special. The fragrant steam rising from the food smells like incense and spice in an Arabian marketplace. I begin to worry.

From her purse Gloria has taken a plastic bag of miniature American flags, and she runs from place setting to setting sticking the toothpick poles into marshmallows also dug from her purse. These novelties are placed in the center of each dish. She charges when she sees us come into the room.

"You must be Bernard's brother Hokum," she says, prying loose Joachim's hand from Lorraine's to pump it. "Isn't this just marvelous, all of us together on this great day. Just imagine, our forefathers sat down to a dinner like this, right here in this very city, two hundred years ago. It makes me feel like I'm part of history."

Joachim's expression is blank but his voice is full of gallantry when he replies to her in Spanish. I don't know the true extent of what he says; I catch only one word— *capitalista*. Of course, my mother doesn't understand him either. She doesn't understand people from New York or Atlanta, for that matter.

"Oh dear," she whispers to Lorraine. "Do you think he wants a Stars and Stripes at his setting? He really wouldn't appreciate it, would he, being a foreigner?"

"Everybody please sit down. The food's getting cold," says Rose.

"Maybe we should leave a copy of the Declaration of Independence on his plate," Lorraine tells Gloria, smiling. It has taken Lorraine a long time to feel comfortable around my mother, to realize she can insult her and get away with it and feel better because of it.

"No, no time for that," Gloria says. She forgets about Joachim. "Oh dear, everyone doesn't have a flag yet."

We take our seats, my father shouting at Gloria to sit down and stop bothering people. By my count there are twenty-nine of us, not including the baby, who is asleep upstairs. Bernie sits between Gloria and Uncle Albie at the middle of the table. Across from them, my father is flanked by Rose on his left, me to the right. At the far end of the table by the fireplace, Joachim and Lorraine are seated among the teenagers and children. The New York Lebanese cousins occupy the opposite pole, silhouettes against the sunset. The rest of the folks fill in the gaps. One of the uncles on my mother's side of the family, Uncle Vince, picks up his wineglass and proposes a toast to the Alazars, and then continues on into grace.

"Dear Lord, our Savior, we thank Thee for our bounty, and we ask Thee to bless this generous home, and to let Your love shine upon it and fill it with happiness and wealth." (My mother barks "Amen" to this.) "And we thank Thee for our good health and for bringing us safely together to rejoice in Your glory and to sing the praise of this great nation. Let us now drink a toast to our forebears; let us salute their forbearance, and never let us forget or cease to honor the courage and the dream of men like George Washington—"

Joachim interrupts him. We get a demonstration of the fireball the stewardesses had warned me about. He picks up a celery stick and points it like a shiv at my surprised uncle.

"Washington could never unbutton his pants by himself," Joachim announces. "Do you know what that means?"

No one dares to answer, although I think I hear the New Yorkers grunt. After a moment, Joachim goes on.

"Hamilton's fingers always stank from playing with his own ass. His father was a Portuguese pimp who washed ashore in the West Indies. I say God bless Tomás Jefferson. He was confused, okay, but he was honest and he knew what men needed. To hell with Lenin and Ike. None of the bastards, not a one, understood Lorenzo of *The Plumed Serpent*. So what did you expect? Eh? *Viva la revolución de los corazones!*"

"Oh my God," says Rose.

"It's okay," Bernie shouts down to Joachim.

"Amen," says Lorraine and starts the soup around a silent, mortified table. Everybody tries to concentrate on the food, to be polite, to forget what they have heard, but I can see that Uncle Vince's fuse is lit and an outburst is imminent. He holds off until everybody has his soup, and then explodes.

"Look here you—" he says, rising up out of his chair to yell at Uncle Joachim. There are tears in the old Trotskyite's eyes; Joachim wipes at them with the cuff of his jacket.

"Why don't you just keep quiet, Vince," my father calmly tells his brother-in-law.

"Hell no, I'm not gonna keep quiet," Vince says. "No tamale-eating scoundrel can come up here to the U.S.A. and blacken the name of the men that made the best country in the world."

"Why don't you just settle down, Vince," my father says. "The old fellow was making a joke, that's all."

Vince looks at his sister Gloria for support, but she is staring at her cucumber soup, probing it with her spoon. Vince slumps back into his chair. I think he owes Dad too much to resist him. He will go only so far for his country; likewise my mother for her family. As far as Gloria is concerned, the interchange never took place. This is her special gift: to blind herself to dissension, diffuse the obvious.

Joachim is stirred by Vince's challenge. He snatches up a butter knife and brandishes it.

"Hey, *gringo*, let me tell you something," he says. "The only thing Columbus ever discovered was the clap."

Vince turns a rather brutal shade of purple, but before he can do anything, Lorraine breaks up with laughter, deep and heartfelt with no edge to it. She tries to take the knife away from Uncle Joachim; he won't give it up. Instead he stretches forward to dip it into hommos, which he spreads on a piece of pita bread. Lorraine laughs louder. Her eyes are closed and I can see she's releasing all the tension that's been building. Bernie joins her, his short, coughing laughs an exclamation to Lorraine's flowing melodies, and I finally wise up myself. Soon we are all laughing and everybody seems to relax a little. Lorraine teases both Vince and Joachim about their hot blood. Gloria finishes exploring her soup.

"This looks marvelous, Rose," she says.

Gloria lifts a spoonful to her shiny lips, blowing to cool it off. She says nothing after she swallows it, but from the expression on her face she might have put a dead fish in her mouth.

"Oh goodness," she says. "How wonderfully different. But everybody's been talking so much it's cooled off."

"It's okay," says Bernie. "Rose makes it for . . ." But the words swim away from him. He works the muscles in his cheeks and jaw in frustration, waiting for the sensation of loss to pass, for redemption, for the tide of his thoughts to return the words. I can see that it is killing him. Gloria has turned expectantly, grateful that Rose's husband is finally speaking to her. Because they do not know better, because in their innocent eyes Bernie is still the head of the household, the Missouri relatives also offer him their formal attention. Lorraine, my father, Uncle Albie, and the cousins from Queens keep right on eating. Something washes up on the shore of Bernie's brain. He is clinging to a lectern, authoritative in his prime, Rose's sweet "professor-type" once again.

"If we are to believe Mr. Dulles," he says, "the Cold War was not the result of imaginary fears or the eagerness of the intelligence community, but of a direct and genuine threat to the security of Europe, and consequently, the United States."

Joachim looks up from his plate. "*Mierda,*" he says. "Forget that crap, Bernie."

Rose comes to Bernie's rescue this time. "I make it especially for hot summer days," she says. Bernie unbends like a man being pulled from a small hole.

"It's so refreshing," my mother lies. "I never would have thought of such a thing myself."

"I think it's great, Rose," says Albie. He shows us an appetite that made him my grandmother's favorite son. Even my father is enthusiastic as he inspects the bowls of tabouleh and couscous, the platters of hot pita and feta cheese, the yogurt, skewers of shish kebab that Rose had Albie grill outside on the patio. My other relatives look on in self-pity. There is nostalgia in their expressions for corn on the cob and country ham. They take complimentary portions of each dish and poke the spoonfuls like children ordered to eat liver and lima beans.

"Where's my hot dog?" one of the kids whines. His mother shushes him.

"Lookit that guy," says another kid, pointing at Uncle Joachim. His head is down over his plate and he stuffs kibbeh into his mouth with all ten fingers. Everybody turns to watch.

"Was your brother born Mexican originally?" Gloria asks Bernie.

"*Landstadt en gimmler pooksny,*" Bernie replies. He has abandoned the English language, or it has forsaken him as if it too can judge when a man no longer needs something. My mother's eyes narrow. She slices at her mouth with a napkin.

"Are you mocking me, Mr. Alazar?" she says icily. "Because if you are, I want you to know that I've just about had enough of these people out here in the East."

"He's sick, you goddamn bitch; you're so blind!" Lorraine screams. She pushes away from the table, looking at me defiantly, but I would applaud her if I could. When she is Rose's daughter, when her Irish blood rises and shows itself, she is stronger than me and I need her to teach me the secret of that power. My father gets up, glares at his wife, and goes to soothe his daughter-in-law. Lorraine excuses herself before he reaches her; the baby probably needs changing, she says, and hurries out of the room. Gloria winces but I know she feels triumphant. She has discovered the leverage that will restore her sense of well-being and confidence.

"I'm so sorry, Rose," she says. "Can you ever forgive me?" Her sympathy is phosphorescent, like certain worms, giving only a dull light and no warmth. I see she plans to say more, but Uncle Albie stops eating, reaches across in front of Bernie, who seems to be meditating, and knocks a glass of red wine off the table into Gloria's lap.

"You wicked pool-hall tramp!" Gloria shrieks. "You did that on purpose!" She looks toward my father for support, but he won't even acknowledge her complaint. The Missouri relatives are frozen, fearful of being attacked if they make the slightest move. The New York Lebanese terrorists are devouring great heaps of food.

"Oh!" Gloria is crying. "Oh, Lord!" An obscene magenta stain expands below the waist of her sky-blue summer dress. She jumps up from her seat and runs out of the room. Uncle Albie excuses himself to make a phone call. Rose seems impassive, under a spell; the kids squirm where they sit. Outside there is a muffled, distant explosion. It is followed by a whistle and then another boom.

"Fireworks!" the kids yell to one another. "Let's go!" They race for the front door and out into the darkness. The aunts and uncles each take a last token nibble of Rose's cooking, congratulate her on its excellence, and apologize for their concern over the children's safety. They, too, then leave the dining room, their chairs scraping guiltily across the hardwood floor. Bernie's cousins remain to finish off the meal.

117

"Stay calm, *amigos*," advises Joachim. "The day has come. We've nothing to worry about. And tomorrow, tomorrow . . ." His voice fades.

Rose looks at him as if she'd like to yank his tongue out. Joachim wipes his hands delicately with his napkin and then proceeds to buff down his fingernails on the stone surface of the hearth, stopping occasionally to check his progress. My father leaves to search out my mother. I suspect he'll have an apology ready by the time he finds her—maybe she deserves one. Rose is not aware that Bernie has also exited. She puts her elbows on the table and her head in her hands, fingers raking the limp hair as if this were a way to exorcise her fears.

"I don't have room for this in my mind," she says, but not to anyone in particular. She looks up in time to see Bernie with his winter coat on, headed for the door.

"Jack," she says. "Don't let him go. Stop him."

I reach the door when he does and have to pry his hand from the knob. His flesh loosens in my grip like a ripe peach. "Where are you going, Bernie?" I ask. He doesn't know. "Why don't you stay here, then, with Joachim?"

"Okay. Sure."

Albie is standing quietly there when we turn around. He is studying Bernie; I feel he wants to say something, but it takes a moment and first he must clear his throat.

"Unless they be like little children," he says, "they shall not find heaven, or something like that. Shit, imagine me trying to quote the Bible."

"My heart is losing gravity," Bernie says. "I can feel it lifting right up."

Albie smiles and nods at him, shakes his head sadly. He says to me, "Look, Jack, explain things to your folks and Rose and Lorraine. I've called a cab to take me out to the Coast. You know how it is."

"Yeah," I agree. "Good seeing you, Uncle Alabard."

"Bernie," he says, taking three cigars from his coat pocket, "here. I want you to have these." Albie turns to me and confides, "I gave him one in the kitchen and he loved it."

I say good-bye and he leaves. The front yard reverberates with the sharp clacks of firecrackers and bottle rockets that my relatives have imported with them from the untamed Midwest. The celebrations shift into high gear.

Someone outside is screaming wildly—whether from pain or great joy, I do not know. Cherry bombs blast from one end of the property to the other and Rose's poodles yelp hysterically. Perhaps big skyrockets are being tied to their collars now for an airborne pooch finale. A barrage of Roman candles sends an aura of multicolored light through the window of the door; it fades across our faces.

I tell Bernie to hang his coat back in the hall closet, but he wants to talk to Joachim first. We shuffle back to the dining room. Bernie's cousins still scrape the serving bowls, but Rose has disappeared. Joachim's fingers are raw and bloodied from rubbing them against the stone.

"And Poppa says, 'What did you catch, Bernie, stinkfish?' And he makes the maid scrub you with lanolin and throw out your clothes to save you from Momma's sensitive nose. You were a great fisherman, Leon."

"It's okay," Bernie says tenderly. He puts his arm around his brother and sits down beside him. I leave the two of them together and hunt for Lorraine. I find her in the upstairs bath. The water is running in the sink, but she won't let me in. She tells me she'll be downstairs in a minute. I wander back toward the dining room, but on the way I hear voices coming from inside the hall closet. I pull back the door and clouds of pungent smoke press into my face. Bernie and Joachim squat on the floor of the big

119

walk-in closet, quietly puffing on the cigars that Albie bequeathed them.

"We're celebrating our reunion," Joachim tells me.

I squeeze in with them. Bernie hands me the last cigar and I light up. Lorraine finds us a few minutes later.

"Jesus Christ, you're going to suffocate in there." She reaches in and flicks on the ventilation fan. In a moment the smoke has cleared. "You want to come out and sit somewhere comfortable?" she asks.

"No," I say. "Come in and close the door behind you."

She slides in with us. Her shirt is lifted and she is nursing the baby. She hands me the kid and puts her arms around her father's neck.

"It's okay," says Bernie.

The only sounds coming from the darkness are the heavy breaths of Joachim, a sigh from Lorraine, the round, milky bird noise of the baby, like a morning song. Outside, the rockets are bursting in air.

for Barbara Azar Davis

THE TRAPDOOR

ONE

Like the unambitious towers of the New World, the playhouses rose before the passengers to a modest height and then stopped unconvincingly. The pilot tied off the skiff to the landing and waited to be paid. The first gentleman out turned back to offer a hand to the lady, lifting her up by the elbow onto the boardwalk stuck into the muddy bankside. Resisting the urge to return with the ferryman to London, Sir Philip's guest, the privateer Captain Relsworth, stood up in the bow of the unstable boat and gracefully leapt ashore, a hand on his rapier to keep it from banging between his legs.

There, like the towers of Santa Marta, of Maracaibo, of Havana, the Captain said to himself, looking up the bank: squat white hives close to the earth, afraid of heaven but brilliant in the afternoon sun, somehow begging faith in their solidness and invulnerability. The Spanish had no time to build proper defenses, no apparent need to build them high. The golden tropic sun ruined one's sense of proportion: Men were not men in the Indies but gods and animals. Drake's culverins had been able to lob nine-pound shot into the towers like a child dropping raisins into a fish basket.

"You see, Captain," Sir Philip said, his palm held out in front of him, "there to the left is the *Globe,* bearing the sign of Atlas, and there the *Rose* in the middle, and there is the bear-baiting ring in the trees, you see?"

The woman had turned, with a coy expression, to witness that the Captain did in fact see, so that she did not know they had come to the end of the boards, where there was a drop to the grass. She missed her step and tripped. The high heel of her shoe snapped off and she would have fallen had she not caught her escort's arm. The Captain frowned. He did not like the ostentatious woman with her affectations, her lemon velvet, her hair dyed pale orange and crisped so that it erupted from her temples, her jewels of colored glass. She was a trull as far as the Captain was concerned. Whether or not the court was willing to acknowledge its demimondaines now that Elizabeth was dead, Sir Philip was still a fool to have such a woman on his arm.

"Oh, la," she was crying. "Wait. I've broken it. We must go back. The louts shall have a laugh at my uneven step."

Sir Philip sought to calm her with sugary words. She stood pouting, raised on her left toes to compensate the loss of her heel. A few forced tears loosened the paint in the corners of her eyes, leaving black-rimmed trails along the sides of her nose. The Captain thought the woman looked and acted absurdly, but he wanted to agree with her, he wanted to return to his office in London and finish the business that had brought him to the city. Sir Philip took her hand and stroked it in a fatherly fashion.

THE TRAPDOOR

"Surely, my lady, this is a small misfortune. The Captain rarely comes to see us. You haven't been to Bankside since before we built the *Fortune,* have you, sir? Ah, surely not. Shall you deny him his pleasure for a heel, my lady?"

"Sir Philip," the Captain began, "my satisfaction would be as great—"

"Tush, sir. Tush! Thou dost not stop a carriage because the horse has muddied itself."

He continued to hold her wrist as if she might run away.

"The groundlings'll whistle at me," she said miserably. "I shall bobble like an old goose."

A flush of choler tightened the features of Sir Philip's face. He lost his patience and demanded her other shoe. The woman stubbornly obeyed, leaning over to pluck it off. The heel and toes of her stocking were mildly soiled. The Captain watched indifferently as Sir Philip took the good shoe and broke the long square wooden heel from it. It cracked like a chicken bone in his hands. The woman made a sound as if she had been pinched. Sir Philip bowed graciously and returned the shoe to its owner.

"There," he said victoriously. "They are equal. I will buy you new ones."

To hide his weak smile, the Captain petted his shiny black mustaches. He wished the woman had had her way. If he must come to Bankside, he would rather attend a bear-baiting. As they walked up the grassy slope, he could smell the beasts' bitter, exciting stench coming from the ring. A gutty snarl crescendoed to a roar, children screamed, and the mastiffs whined and bayed in their blood lust. Was that a lion? he wondered. Didn't they sometimes have lions on Sundays? He would like to see *that,* by God. That would be a story to tell his men.

They were coming up to the horses. The white pins of jugglers spun in the sky beyond where the animals grazed.

Somewhere someone was strumming a lute or cittern, he couldn't decide which. If there were music, the Captain thought, he could endure the afternoon. Music or beasts, but not, for God's sake, speeches. The woman, much smaller now without her heels, ordered one of the horse-boys to remove his charge away from the footpath. He made an ugly face at her but complied, tugging the massive, liver-colored stallion farther down the lawn. The Captain thought, I should spring up on its back without a word to Sir Philip and gallop down the lonely green roads to Plymouth, back to the sea. He would rather be in Plymouth, where his ship was being careened and its hull tallowed for speed than waste an afternoon watching players beat the air for a horde of twitching landsmen. He belonged back there, overhauling the gear and refitting the rigging with his crew. Or sitting in the *Salt and Sugar* on the sea-slapped quay, the seagulls rioting over scraps on the cobbles while he drank the rum he himself had pirated from the Spanish.

He would most like to be back on the sea, where he had spent his life, where the wind did not smell like the gutters of London or a gallant's perfume, where he was not servant but a master in the most masterful fleet on the globe. Better there than here in London, where the fashions changed in a fortnight and a soberly dressed gentleman was treated as a foreigner. He was weary of the clucking of Sir Philip and his Providence Company and their misinformed rush to colonize, to follow Spain's lead. Years ago Raleigh had proven the madness of that course. Like the clergyman's *Gloria Patri,* the word *gold* shaped the lips of every agent on Fleet Street into a round prayer. There was no more gold, save where the Spanish were. The crown's treasury had been fattened through piracy and slaving and trade. Now oily-haired men who had never set a finger on a nautical chart talked as if the New World were paradise. If it was, it wasn't a place for an Englishman to live unless he was raised naked and senseless. God knew Ireland was full of savages; let them populate the hellish jungles, the frozen marshes. No, the Captain decided, the merchants would never lure *gentlemen* there. As for himself, he would always return upon the mercy of the Lord to the roses of England, the exquisite white puffs and red daubs, delicate as the heart of a virgin.

Aye, he told himself, either the British coast or the heaving of the sea—but here, they were entering the tower. Sir Philip was passing a shilling for a gentlemen's box. The Captain resigned himself to Sir Philip's love of the players.

TWO

It was a large cage for birds too occupied with each other or impressed by their own finery to fly out the unbarred top. Perched in two tiers around and above him, coxcombs and courtiers and Fleet Street moneymen pushed toward their seats, creating a reeling spectrum of queer colors—cornflower blue and magenta like a spray of fuchsia, a lusty, improper yellow, pease-porridge tawny, green and silver stripes, popish reds. Here and there in the flock ostrich-like ladies twisted and bounced, the gray and scarlet plumes of their headdresses swaying above them, their hips made mighty with wire hoops. The yard to his side, for Sir Philip had led them to a box at stage-right on the ground level, was like a marketplace spinning with East End cockneys and drunkards, weaselish fops in the most eccentric styles, beggars, bullies, and hucksters peddling apples, hard pears, rock sugar, chestnuts, and beer, or advertising less honorable entertainments that would commence at dusk in Soho.

125

Sir Philip hailed a fat, unhappy man who sold them wine of questionable quality. Still people squeezed into the pit. The Captain surveyed the thousands of playgoers with disgust. The masses carried the plague on their tongues and spit it into the stale air. He did not particularly enjoy crowds unless he had license to beat at them with a stick or cutlass. He was hot and uncomfortable and drank his wine quickly to relieve his spleen. Their party had not arrived early enough and they were forced to share the box with two men who played monte bank on square boards set across their knees. Sir Philip, who had sat down next to them, greeted them coolly, suspicious of their common blouses. The Captain felt trapped between the woman and Sir Philip, who sat rigid and focused, as though someone were painting his portrait. Long metallic curls of hair spread like coils of ash on the starched surface of his ruff, and his beard lay out on it like a sleeping dog. The Captain did not share this urbane fondness for shackling one's neck in the stiff, hideous things, propping up the layers with forks and wires—a clean linen collar or a simple mantle were genteel enough. The single indulgence the Captain permitted himself was a gold cross earring he had torn from the lobe of a *hidalgo,* a *son of something,* on a pinnace they had captured off the shores of Tortuga.

The woman was restless. With every breath she took she shuffled or wriggled, straightened her neck in its high collar or jerked her hips to find the position they wanted, and every movement she made caused the gold and white tissue of her skirt to crackle. The closeness of the woman nauseated the Captain. She had doused her breast and shoulders generously with lilac perfume, a scent he abhorred for its sweetness, but through the disguise of lanolin her fingers smelled of fish when earlier he had kissed her hand. The Captain took a slender white clay pipe from a pocket in his cape, tamped it with tobacco he carried in a leather pouch, and struck a flame to the bowl. His head swelled. The blend he smoked was a gift from a Carib chieftain. The Captain let the heavy smoke curl from his mouth, filling his mustaches and nose with its penetrating aroma. He felt better, his melancholy rounding off to a narcotic glow, mild and pleasant.

Sir Philip suddenly abandoned his pose and placed a hand on the Captain's broad back, tilting over to speak in his ear. A trumpet sounded before the words were out and he pulled away.

"Mark that," he said with good humor. "The first toot! The players are ready, God bless them."

The Captain looked up to the hut on top the tall, narrow house that closed the stage from behind. The call had come from above. The stage resembled a portico; two painted columns rose from the outer corners and supported a high canopy that partially obstructed his view, but he had seen the silver flash of a trumpet up there against the circle of blue sky held by the roof's thatching. Some of the crowd had begun to cheer.

Sir Philip continued with what he had wanted to say. It was a matter of business, as the Captain suspected, a clucking reprimand in praise of thrift: Provision the ship with beer in place of wine, less fresh fruit, less beef, less dried mutton, and more grains. Without expression, the Captain replied he was tight enough. Frugality was an absolute on the uncertain world of the water, but he would not cause his men to increase their natural sufferance. A request for higher crew wages abruptly stalemated the discussion.

The woman decided she had eaten enough of an apple and pitched the core into the yard, hitting, intentionally it seemed, a man who wore a short green jerkin with multi-colored ribbons sewn across the chest. He slowly turned and acknowledged the woman with a wicked smile, showing teeth blackened by a taste for molasses.

" 'Tis Richard Kinch," she said. "I shall never forgive his manners. Oh, stay! He's coming over. He is a fop, a stroller, a wag, a roistering vagabond. Go away, you."

She leaned over the rail of the box to scold him in a voice full of invitation. Sir Philip did not tolerate this for long. He hauled her back beside him, perhaps too firmly, for she protested and he was compelled to kiss her cheek. The Captain marveled at the brashness of so public a kiss. The second trumpet sounded. The two strangers in the box put away their deck of cards and untied leather cases shoved beneath the bench, taking out leaves of paper, a bundle of quills, and two flat bottles of ink stopped with corks.

The Captain had emptied his flagon of wine and called for another, carefully counting out the copper pennies. The vanity that fluttered about, the Spanish lace, the French embroidery and pendants, the pompous German cuts, the Morisco gowns and loose Barbary sleeves adapted from the Turks—this misadventure in taste, this bastard sartorial rainbow had begun to amuse him. To the Captain, the crowd was all parrots and peacocks, gallant, plumed, primped, and feathered creatures that must even wing and pinion the shoulders of doublets and hop about like birds that had never flown. The Italians understood dignity in dress. There was enough color and perfect design in the world without mocking God's creation—*there was the third blast*—and thank heaven that between reason and passion there was only one London.

The clear trumpet note died away to shouting and full applause. At each end of a black arras stretched across the back of the stage, doors opened and a player advanced. The two men met in the middle of the stage and bowed. A boy followed behind them, turning out along the balustrade at the perimeter. He stood to the audience across the way from Sir Philip's party, holding up a painted board.

"Elsinore!" shouted that part of the crowd. The word echoed out over the Bankside. The Captain waited until the boy had circled the stage and faced their box. "Elsinore," the Captain read aloud, satisfied. He liked the Danes. They were a sensible, clear-headed people. He could trust them at sea.

THREE

"My father's ghost will not speak, nor wave his arm like this one," the Captain whispered. He had gripped the oak railing of the box and sat forward until his ruddy face and knuckles were in the plane of the retiring sunlight.

"What dost thou say?" asked Sir Philip politely.

" 'Tis nothing, sir. The play has found me."

"Ah! Though art entwined in the illusion," Sir Philip said proudly, as though he were responsible for the Captain's earnest attention.

The ghost rising from the center of the stage had chilled the mariner's heart. It wore rusty armor wrapped in a loose gauze of black muslin, a mist of the underworld. Its face was a terrible white in which the eyes were desperate islands, and a snowy beard splashed down the front of its corselet like a waterfall. Up from hell the phantom rose, a menace to the living, and then vanished behind the arras, reappearing when the third man joined the soldiers of the Danish King. Against the Captain's will, the apparition lifted up from deep within him, carrying with it the ghost of his own father. Just as the groundlings strained forward or shoved back from the stage in morbid attraction or dread, his mind worked against itself to foil the vision as it leached through the void. But then cannon firing from above in the tower house had sent it back to its hole.

Now once more the thing drifted out from the black curtain, reaching into his past, his blood bolting through him like a school of frightened mullet—*into every brain that looks so many fathoms to the sea and hears it roar beneath*—and he watched transfixed as the ghost and Hamlet (whose first entrance had caused the woman to swoon with the name *Burbage* on her lips) confronted one another at the edge of their gallery—*if thou dids ever thy dear father love*—where the Prince looked to throw his arms around the unnatural form of the dead King, his father—*Revenge his foul and most unnatural murder*—but embraced only the night air of the battlement.

Oh, horrible! O, horrible! most horrible!
Adieu, adieu, adieu! remember me.

He had forgotten. How many years now had it been? Fourteen? Fifteen? Fifteen this month, was it? He had been holding his breath through the scene, it seemed, and exhaled wearily, returning from the rail to sit upright on the bench, the sea foaming beneath him. My father's ghost never spoke to me, the Captain repeated to himself, and no one else would swear to seeing it.

It had followed him over the oceans to the West Indies and to Panama, to Cathay and Tartary and the Northern Territories, through the Straits of Magellan, pulling it together out of the moist night, knitting the wind and fog into a familiar shape, bent as it once was with dysentery, long cheekbones drawing the face into sadness, a luminescent grief.

The Captain had been a young cannoneer on Frobisher's flagship when the Armada was first sighted off Plymouth in 1588. His father had been a Lieutenant Commander with Drake on the *Revenge*. For years, the Queen had managed her navy scandalously. She had failed to provide her sailors with ammunition and denied their wages with the shake of a jeweled glove. Meat and wine were replaced with a pauper's fare of peas and saltfish, rancid oil and old beer. Men were rotting as they fought, his father among them, thinned and pale beyond the son's recognition.

The first day there was a westerly wind, the seas pushing higher and higher as night fell. The Armada lined the horizon like an eagle with outstretched wings, bloody in the sunset. In the morning Frobisher, the Welch mystic, set upon them with his necromancy, dipping like a sparrow, there and gone before the Spanish could come about, stinging the slow galleons with well-aimed broadsides. At dusk in heavy seas that scattered them, the Spanish fleet ran up-channel for Calais, the Queen's ships in pursuit. Drake was in the lead, bearing the lantern. But without signaling, he had broken off with the *Bear* and *Mary Rose* to prey upon stragglers. At sunrise Sunday, the unsuspecting English saw that the light off their bows was not the *Revenge* but a galleon. They were in the center of the Spaniards but quickly jibed. Frobisher and the other admirals reconnoitered at a safe distance, returning to pluck one by one—like feathers from a bird, Sir Hawkins had said—the ships of the Armada. They did not see the *Revenge* that day; by nightfall the boy had learned that Drake had captured the disabled *Catalina*, her four hundred men and fifty-five thousand ducats. The boy's father was among the boarding party.

On Tuesday, with a change of wind to the south-southwest, Drake rejoined them and they fought the Spanish together throughout the unending week. For the young cannoneer, the world around him was broken and reduced

131

to salt and blood and flame in the wooden vault of his post. He felt he must die than fight another day; his hands, chest, and face were covered with black blisters from the heat of the gun. But by the week's end the Armada was decimated and the Lord Admiral knighted Frobisher. In port the boy borrowed a skiff and rowed over to the *Revenge*. His father was not aboard. None of the crew had seen him since the capture of the *Catalina*. He assumed his father was lost in action. No, he was told, the galleon had surrendered without resistance. That night Frobisher accused Drake of treason for refusing to divide the *Catalina*'s gold among the fleet. The boy lay awake in his hammock wondering if his father were in heaven or hell.

The Captain had forgotten the love he still held for his father until this moment, unexpectedly pushed forward through a passage that had closed in his memory, into a revelation of the fleshless remains of his father and his own torn being where the true life of a man was a stage amusement for which you paid a shilling. The Captain's emotion seemed to squirt out onto his tongue.

"Aye, revenge!" he shouted to the actors. It was a burst of tropical suddenness that soon evaporated. He quickly sat back, silent and remote, surprised by himself.

Sir Philip was stirred by the Captain's show of enthusiasm. The play was a revival; he had attended an earlier performance at Oxford when the children took over Blackfriars Inn. Sir Philip felt the need to point out the *significance,* the hidden meaning, of the production to the Captain.

"They say," he said with authority, "that our own headless Essex and Southampton formed the mold of this Hamlet and Horatio, and Leicester's the treacherous pretender."

The Captain nodded his head blankly, uninterested,

struggling to concentrate on the players through the gaps in his consciousness where the seas rushed madly over the image of his father. Sir Philip had noticed the blood come into his guest's sunburnt face, staining it dangerously bright. He hailed a wine vendor, fearing an attack of apoplexy in the Captain.

The woman's attention was circling the play; she was intrigued for the moment by the noblemen in the surrounding galleries. Her focus, however, would always return to Hamlet. She wondered how she might persuade Sir Philip to introduce her to Burbage, whom he often drank with. The two peculiar men at the end of their box annoyed the financier, yet he could not help but notice them. Each man was mouthing the words a second after the actors, scribbling intrepidly in what appeared to Philip to be a code of some sort on sheet after sheet of paper which mounted on the floor. The Captain too had glanced over earlier and seen them bent across their boards, lips moving in silent recitation, the quill pens skipping and gliding like flying fish. They had drawn a circle with a dot in its center when the word *gold* was spoken by a player. Sir Philip stared in vexation at the pages filled with broken symbols, a milieu of frozen insects with legs sticking every which way. What language is that? he asked them. But they didn't look up from their work.

The Captain was studying the ghost. It was leaving, dropping from sight in the middle of the stage. The Captain felt shame. It was true; until this moment his father wasn't even a memory, only a shadow he would turn from at sea many years ago.

FOUR

He gave the third *adieu—remember me*—and ducked his head under the stage too quickly, bumping the crown of his helmet.

He hurried, but it was difficult to move with sureness or grace in the heavy armor. Crouching halfway down the ladder, he pulled at the trapdoor to set it back in place, closing himself in darkness. He called softly for the stage boys, but no one answered so he continued backing down the steps unassisted. His foot missed the last rung: a wrench of the ankle in its soft inner boot, and pain as he crashed down onto the dirt. A groan followed, venomous cursing under his breath. Where were the boys? He wished them boils on their arse, snakes in their bed, chancres on their lips. He even swore at his foot as if he could insult away the injury. Ghosts should not have to crawl back to the tiring-house.

"My lord?" It was a pretty voice.

"My lord, indeed, my lord! Thy lord and master. Where are thou, boy? Must thou hide to play dice?"

The ghost's eyes adjusted to the weak light filtering through the black curtains that enclosed the base of the stage. In the outermost corner he could see a silhouette rise and move hesitantly toward him through the forest of oaken supports.

"My lord, art thou hurt?"

"Come up, boy. Thou art sluggish enough." The weight of his voice drew the figure onward. The ghost lifted off his helmet. It scraped his ears.

"God-a-mercy! Who is this in a maiden's costume?"

"A maiden, sir."

"Marry, a maiden! A rare thing in London since our Queen has left the world to wed our Lord, if He suits her."

THE TRAPDOOR

"A woman then, and not so rare."

"Ah, a woman, God's grace to you. Art thou named, woman, or dost a man call only 'woman' to call thee?"

"Virginia Fields, my lord."

"And why dost thou crouch down here with the devil?"

" 'Tis a fitting place as any, sir, for a woman—to be underneath and the world above."

"Why, well said! You are not so simple," he said, in praise of her defiant words. "Mark! The cue. I have forgotten the actors." He pulled himself off his elbows to a sitting position and bellowed, *Swear,* startling the girl. His round, bald forehead shimmered like a moon in the gloom around them. *Swear!* he yelled again in a mock deep voice that made the girl snort with suppressed laughter.

"Nay, be quiet. Take this headpiece and thump it thrice on the bottom of the front stage so that it rings. Wait till I speak."

She moved off into the shadows while he carefully listened to the faint words above. She had to stoop to keep from bumping her head on the trusses. There was the cue again. He hissed at the girl to warn her.

Swear by his sword.

She banged against the floorboards.

"Psst. Holla, lady. Enough!" She groped her way back to him.

"I pray you, dear Lady Fields, sweet angel of this cave, the unlighted belly of the world, pull this iron from my chest. The buckles line the side."

She was charmed by his flattery but still timid, afraid to come too close. He seemed like a gentleman, but she knew how sudden the mood of a man could change. Even in the poor light she could sense an ambiguity in his hard eyes that the sun would not affect. He peeled off his beard. Underneath were clean cheeks and a perfect chin. Then he put his head back as though he were trying to swallow the muffled noises that sank down to him from the stage.

"Once again," he whispered hoarsely. And then, *Swear!*

"More!" she cried. "My lord, the stage master has punished thee."

"How so?"

"He must loathe thy face and company to cast thee in a role so lonely and distant from the surface. Thou art on the wrong side for men to appreciate thy talent."

"Aye, I must speak to him about my position, and tell the gatekeeper to hold a better seat for thee tomorrow."

"Thanks, my lord," she said, despondent. "Shall you swear again?"

"No more."

He lifted his arms and she knelt by him and pried the breastplate from his chest, forcing it open like a clamshell. Off came the girdle of mail, the brassards, the thigh guards, and finally from his shins the steel jambs, tossed aside in the dirt. Underneath it all he was dressed in galligaskins and garter stockings and a cambric blouse. He stretched forward to rub his ankle. Now that she had finished, she turned away, forgetting him for a more portentous matter. Unexpectedly he was stern and she cringed as he assumed a manner of formality.

"Hast thou seen my boys?"

"Too much."

"A short and bitter fact you make it. Where did they wander?"

"I know not, my lord."

"Prithee, go and call them."

"No, my lord."

"What's this! You'd make a beggar of me?"

"No, my lord. I cannot go. I am banished like thee to hell."

THE TRAPDOOR

There was a flourish of trumpets from above them. The girl jumped up and cocked her head to listen. She began to rapidly suck in air until she could contain no more and exhaled weeping.

"There he is! Oh, I cannot bear it."

"Shhh. Who?"

"My heart."

"Where?"

"Atop us. Mark that voice. Thy Queen!"

"My Queen? Surely not."

"Aye, thy Queen. Hamlet's mother, Gilly Nashe—the King's boy. Your duckling about to break his egg. Mark that voice with the sap rising to it. His hour upon the stage shall soon end. He has outgrown his skirts and grown a beard, and I have gained his loss."

"Thy wit is pregnant, lady. You give me pause."

"My wit? Nay, sir. My belly."

Out of despair, she fell down beside him, the tears running again, her forehead braced against his shoulder. He tried to comfort the wretched child, patting her back as he would his own daughter, embarrassed. Though language was the water he most liked to swim in, he could think of nothing to say to her. Then her spirit seemed to shift; she was herself again, and angry.

"And thy same Gilly's—my Gilly's—soft words have caused it."

"Words! I think not, lady. They lack the proper essence."

"Nay, my lord, words were enough. For two years he has courted me, and swore he would marry at the season's close. 'Ginny, my flower, my rose, let me taste once from this table,' says he, pulling my buttons, 'or I shall surely starve.' He took his fill, my lord, but now he's abused my trust and innocence. I came at midday to greet him and

threw my arms around his neck to kiss the untimely news
into his ear. He broke away from me as if I had bit him and
forbid my presence at the playhouse. I ran to hide my grief
and found shelter in the dimness here, and had fixed my
mind to kill myself when I heard a coarse oath about
snakes and such and found thee in the dirt growling."

"Go to—kill thyself!"

"Aye. Nay, I shall kill him instead."

"A husband would be more fitting than an angel, child.
Seek to impress him with his obligation and, one hopes,
love, rather than lift him beyond it."

"He's thick-hearted, my lord."

A door creaked and footsteps cluttered down the stairs
from the tiring-house. Two indistinct figures stumbled
about the murky chamber, calling his name. It was Nozzle
and Harry come to find him. Their boyish faces loomed
out of the shadows.

"Ho, stop there or you'll walk on us."

"Master? Ah, hallo. Henslowe said to discover what
became of thee. Oh, in faith, sir. We did not know you
were so engaged, now did we, Nozzle? Your pardon, sir,
we pray you."

They started to fade back into darkness.

"Stay, Harry. Give me your hand. I've bruised my foot
and can't step on it. The lady's acquainted with our
boy-Queen Gilly."

The stage boys looked closer, recognizing the girl. They
had often seen her hanging on Gilly Nashe, and Gilly on
her. They straddled the ghost and raised him, his arms
wrapped over their shoulders, the rest of his weight shifted
to his left foot.

"Farewell, my lord. Thanks for your charitable ear."

"Nay, come with us, Virginia. Hurry, while your
boy-man's still on stage. We'll fashion a plot to set a vision

of conscience into Gilly. Pray, follow. He cannot stay Queen forever."

"He has proved that."

Their entrance backstage in the tiring-house was little noticed through the urgent confusion that is natural to such a place. The narrow room smelled of grease and sweaty wool and talc. Players hurried to change costumes wherever they could find space in makeshift stalls between props and racks of clothes. For the girl, coming here was like entering an alchemist's workshop, where simple specimens of humanity like herself could be refashioned into a king, a queen, a Moor, a great lover, or a witch. Only she was a woman, something less than these simple men, and the magic of acting was taboo to her sex. Her bleak fate weakened her and she wanted to stop, but the wounded ghost, in a kind and tender manner, urged her forward past the thrones and chairs and stools, sets of armor like the one he himself had left underneath the stage, into a thicket of halberds and lances ornamented with streamers and out again into a passage hung with caps and bonnets and headdresses on which feathers waved and bristled from a breeze that gusted through an open window. Then a row of coat stands hanging with robes, silk and velvet and fur-trimmed, purchased from the servants of dead nobility. Despite the visual busyness, every human motion was dreamlike, folded up and hidden in silence; the unseen presence of something greater seemed to press upon it all and soften the texture without diminishing it.

He was all right, he insisted, and dismissed the boys back to their duties after Harry had brought him a crutch. The girl waited for him while he hopped one-legged to speak with a man who sat on a stool by the stage-right entrance, shuffling through a mound of papers in his lap. The man listened with a puzzled expression on his face to her benefactor's instructions, trying to understand what it was his ghost wanted. He leaned over and pulled down the actor's stocking to inspect the puffy ankle. Then, with soundless, shaking laughter, the man seemed to consent, and the ghost hobbled back to her with a luster in his eyes.

She followed him to a small anteroom behind a vertical stack of lumber. He quickly urged her forward and shut the door behind them. Moments later someone was tentatively knocking at it. She gasped when she heard the voice and put her hands over her mouth.

"Master, are you fit? Henslowe says you have lamed your foot."

"Go away, Gilly, while I pray for quick healing. You'll see me in the closet scene."

The ghost did not know who was right, or how the matter finally should be settled. Perhaps the girl was a strumpet, but he didn't think so. Gilly must confront the issue nevertheless. And here was a fine test for Burbage's courage and greatness, a diversion to complement their ale afterward at the Boar's Head. He called the girl over to a chair behind his writing table. In the light she was not pretty, nor unpleasing. Her dark appearance, her man's nose, her fat cheeks and small bosom, but ah, he noticed, those lively eyes would not lack suitors in hungry London, and her wit was not easily matched. She was of the type that, dressed in the right clothes, would attract wealth and station.

"Remove thy slippers and put these heeled boots on to raise thee. Do they fit?"

"Nay."

"No matter. You shall not walk far with them."

"My lord?"

"Aye?"

"The stage-master will not allow your game."

"I think not, Virginia. 'Tis my play, and mine to play with."

Her dress was straight and plain, without the layers of petticoats or architecture of a farthingale to swell it out like a pumpkin. She would not have to remove it.

"Now, my lady," he said, catching up her long auburn hair, "let me tie this back with a ribbon. None shall know thee save those that know thee closely."

FIVE

The music startled him back into the play. The stretching moan of the sackbuts was like a fat finger pressing in to his emotions. The plaintive bass viol deepened the sense of loss that had been hounding him since he had seen the ghost. He would rock on the sea for months with never the desire to stand and check himself in front of a looking glass, but here he must sit idly by and watch men full of airy gestures and long speeches open him up and unsettle his peace. He had never been a man of words, of lady-pleasing or beguiling phrases. His course was sudden and deliberate action, as was England's. Hamlet's indecisiveness challenged him; the man's defective will burned against the Captain's instinct. The Dane was casting his father deeper into diabolic misery. And Sir Philip obviously approved.

"Hamlet's a fool." The Captain sneered. "He's content to tease the villain with a troop of loobies. Now the tragedy will double."

"Don't believe so hastily," said Sir Philip. "Hamlet is a man of cunning humor. He'll trip the King with cords of distraction."

"Hamlet finds no difference between the nut and the shell. The part he pretends is real; thus there is no pretending, but a wind that blows from all directions."

141

Sir Philip paused to think about this. The Captain jumped up before he could reply.

"Mark that! The visiting players have set a fire under the King—he flees and all doubt follows. Mark that, I say. If Hamlet is a fox, let him bite. After him, man. What, he stays. God save thee, he only wants to hear his words match each other."

The Captain swung one leg over the railing of the box. This effort mortified Sir Philip and he grabbed the hem of the Captain's tabard.

"Here, where are you going?"

The Captain was not sure.

"I beseech you, sit back, sir. Let the amusement run its course."

There was a growing noise in the pit. Several groundlings clambered up the balustrade of the stage as the King exited. Burbage still strutted about behind the milieu, taking pleasure in responding to catcalls. Rosencrantz and Guildenstern marshaled the intruders from the stage. The Captain sat down with a sigh. After a moment there was music again, bird sounds puffed out of recorders. The sun now divided the stage in half. The Captain blew his swollen nose vigorously into a silk handkerchief and bought more wine, regretting that this was not his fight, more eager than ever to get back to sea. Sir Philip remained fascinated by the men in the corner of their box, still hoping to decipher their code. He imagined they were spies, Knights of Malta, collecting information on the Providence Company. Perhaps later he would have them arrested. The woman had been teary ever since Hamlet first spoke to Ophelia. She dabbed at her eyes with a scarf tied to her wrist. "How brutal," she said under her breath, "his love is."

THE TRAPDOOR

SIX

The Captain's second sense had alerted him. He felt the tension of blood ready to be released. There was a strike, and the old milkweed Polonius fell from behind the arras dead. There's the first. There was no stopping it now. The Captain was satisfied. He was accustomed to and strengthened by danger, sensitive to plans gone astray; his life depended on intuition. The ghost had reappeared and something felt wrong, off balance. The Queen was behaving oddly. The person subdued within the actor seemed to show himself, to jut out for a moment like a white knee through the folds of a robe.

SEVEN

The beard itched and the paint felt like mud on her face. The boots he had made her wear were like pails strapped around her feet. She crossed the stage, clumping each foot down, thinking she must throw her arms around Gilly, but he was backstroking away from her, and Burbage had slid between them. She froze from the clarity of the actor's eyes, the impatience of his mouth. She thought she must run offstage, but then he smiled and seemed to bow slightly in acknowledgment:

A king of shreds and patches—Burbage stopped, licked his lips and howled,

"Risen in a most unnatural form," he added with a wink;

Save me, and hover o'er me with your wings,

You heavenly guards! What would your gracious figure!

Alas, he's mad, said the Queen, but her voice broke in a mulish tone like a viola da gamba stroked with an unresined bow. She grabbed at her throat, stunned, and sat back unladylike on her bed.

Hamlet spoke to the ghost of his father:

Do you come your tardy son to chide,
That, lapsed in time and passion lets go by
Th' important acting of your dread command?
O, say!

Her beard bobbed up and down, but her lips were speechless. The words roared out in a familiar voice from behind the curtain:

Do not forget this visitation
Is but to whet thy almost blunted purpose.
But, look, amazement on thy mother sits:
Speak to her, Hamlet.
How is it with you, lady?

The Queen did not stir. She had pitched back on the bed and was staring wall-eyed at the signs of the Zodiac that whirled about the stage's canopy.

EIGHT

He beckoned the girl offstage. The crutch pinched his underarms, but the sensation vanished as he listened to his Hamlet. Burbage could not be bully-goated, he could not stumble. Given the opportunity he would wag his tongue at anything, and each spontaneous phrase was a miracle of rhythm and concise beauty. Since the Queen would not finish her lines, Burbage was full of wordplay, floating the plot on a tide of wit. The world stopped to hear his fluency. Behind the curtain, the ghost listened quietly to the flowering of the language, musical and complete, as though it had always existed, and would forever.

SQUiRRELLY'S GROUPER

A fish story is like any other, never about a fish but always about a man and a place. I wouldn't even mention it if I thought everybody knew. When you cut down to the bone of the matter, a fish is just Pleasure with a capital P. Rule of thumb—the bigger the fish, the bigger the pleasure. That's one side of the coin of fishing, the personal best and finest, but this is Hatteras, and there's that other side. On the Outer Banks of North Carolina, you can't pitch a rock in the air in the morning without rock-throwing becoming widespread ruthless competition by the time the sun goes down over Pamlico Sound, and that is because we go to sea for our living, and because commercial fishermen think they are God's own image of male perfection. I've seen it go on all my life here on the coast, each generation afflicted with the same desire to lord, bully, and triumph; doesn't even matter where they come from once they're here, north or south or bumbled in from Ohio and beyond like Willie Striker. So that's the other side, where size counts, wakes the sleepyheads right up, subdues the swollen-head gang, and becomes everybody's business.

⚓

We saw the boats off that morning like we always do, and near an hour later Mrs. Mitty Terbill came in the marina store to post a sign she had made, a little gray cardboard square she had scissored from the back of a cereal box. It said: LOST DOG. YORKSHIRE TERRIER. NAME—PRINCE ED, MY SOLE COMPANION. REWARD, and then a number to reach her at.

"What's the reward, Mitty?" I asked. It was five dollars, which is about right for a Yorkie, measured by appeal per pound. Mitty Terbill is not an upright-standing woman, but then considerable woe has befallen her and keeps her squashed into her pumpkin self, allowing for only brief religious ascension. She spent that much plus tax on a twelve-pack and trudged back out the door, foot-heavy in her fishwife's boots, going back to her empty house on the beach to sit by the phone. Well, this story's not about the widow Terbill, though plenty of stories are since she lost her old man and her dope-pirate offspring two Januarys ago when they ran into weather off Cape May, up there flounder fishing I believe it was. That's just how I remember the day settling down after the dawn rush, with Mitty coming in, some of the fellows cracking jokes about how one of the boys must have mistook Prince Ed for bait and gone out for shark, and although Mitty likes her opinions to be known and gets the last word in on most events, let me please go on.

Life is slack at a marina between the time the boats go out early and vacationers get burnt off the beach about noon and come round to browse; then in the afternoons all hell breaks when the boats return. Anyway, after Mitty stopped in, Junior left to pull crab pots; Buddy said he's driving out to Cape Point to see if the red drum are in on the shoals with the tide change; Vickilee took a biscuit breakfast over to her cousins at the firehouse; Albert went down to the Coast Guard station to ingratiate himself to uniformed men; Brainless was out at the pumps refueling his uncle's trawler so he could get back to the shrimp wars, which left just me, my manager Emory Plum, and my two sacked-out Bay Retrievers in the place when I hear what might be an emergency broadcast on the citizen's band, because it's old grouch Striker calling J.B. on channel seventeen. Willie Striker has been one to spurn the advancement of radio and the charity of fellow captains, not like the other jackers out there bounced wave to wave on the ocean. They yammer the livelong day, going on like a team of evangelical auctioneers about where the fish aren't to be found, lying about how they barely filled a hundred-pound box, complaining how there's too many boats these days on the Banks and too many Yankees on land, in a rage because the boys up in Manteo are fetching a nickel more for yellowfin, and who messed with who, and who's been reborn in Christ, and who knows that college girl's name from Rodanthe, and who's going to get theirs if they don't watch it. Willie Striker has something to say himself, but you wouldn't find him reaching out. He kept to himself and preferred to talk that way, to himself, unless he had a word for his wife, Issabell. Keeping to himself was no accident, and I'll tell you why if you just hold on.

J.B. J.B. . . . come in, Tarbaby, I hear, and even though an individual's voice coming through the squawk box fizzes like buggy tires on a flooded road, you know it's Willie Striker transmitting because his words had the added weight of an accent, nothing much, just a low spin or bite on some words. Like mullet, Willie Striker would say, *maul*-it.

Tarbaby Tarbaby . . . come in. That was the name of J.B.'s workboat.

I was restocking baits, ballyhoo and chum, my head bent into the freezer locker, and Emory, he was back behind the counter studying delinquent accounts. "Turn her up a bit there, Emory," I told him, "if you please."

He didn't need to look to do it, he's done it so many times. He just reached behind and spun the dial to volume nine, put a hailstorm and a fifty-knot blow between us and the boats. "Well, who's that we're listening to?" Emory yelled out. "That's not our Mr. Squirrel, is it?"

Some twenty-five years it'd been I guess that Willie Striker had lived among us, married Issabell Preddy, one of our own, came south it was said sick and tired of Dayton and a factory job, and from the day he showed his jumpy self at Old Christmas in Salvo, folks called Striker Squirrelly. If you've seen his picture in the paper, you might think you know why. Squirrelly's got a small shrewd but skittish face with darting, then locking, eyes, a chin that never grew, some skinny teeth right out in the front of his mouth, and his upper lip was short, tight, some called it a sneer. The top of his head was ball-round and bald up to the crown, then silver hair spread smooth like fur. But like any good made-up name that fits and stays, there was more to it than manner of appearance.

Way-of-life on Hatteras Island has long been settled, that's just the way it is. A couple dozen families like mine, we lived together close back to Indian times, wreckers and victims of wrecks, freebooters and lifesavers, outcasts and hermits, beachcombers and pound netters and cargo ferrymen, scoundrels and tired saintly women, until they put the bridge across Oregon Inlet not long after Willie moved down. Outsiders meant complications to us one way or another; the truth is we don't take to them very well—which used to have significance but doesn't anymore, not since the herd stampeded in the last ten years to buy up the dunes and then bulldoze the aquifer. That's the island mascot these days, the yellow bulldozer, and the Park Service rules the beach like communists. That's one thing, but the fact is Willie Striker wouldn't care and never did if a Midgett or a Burrus or a Foster ever said, "Fine day, iddn't Skipper" to him or not. He wasn't that type of man, and we weren't that type of community to look twice at anything unless it had our blood and our history, but Issabell Preddy was the type of woman inwardly endeared to signs of acceptance, which you could say was the result of having a drunkard father and a drunkard mother. Issabell and her brothers went to live with their Aunt Betty in Salvo until they finished school, but Betty had seven children of her own, a husband who wouldn't get off the water, and no time to love them all. I went to school with Issabell and have always known her to be sweet in a motionless way, and not the first on anybody's list. She had one eye floating and purblind from when her daddy socked her when she was small, wore hand-down boys' clothes or sack dresses on Sundays, her fuzzy red hair always had a chewed-on aspect about it, and her skin was such thin milk you never saw her outside all summer unless she was swaddled like an Arab. Back then something inside Issabell made her afraid of a good time, which made her the only Preddy in existence with a docile nature, and the truth is a quiet girl who is no beauty is like a ghost ship or a desert isle to the eyes of young and active men: No matter how curious you are you don't want to be stuck on it.

One by one Issabell's brothers quit school and took off,

joined the Navy and the Merchant Marines, and Issabell herself moved back down the road to Hatteras, rented the apartment above the fishhouse and got employed packing trout, prospered modestly on the modest fringe, didn't hide herself exactly but wouldn't so much as sneeze in company without written invitation. The charter fleet was something new back then; there were not-unfriendly rumors that Issabell upon occasion would entertain a first mate or two during the season. These rumors were not so bad for her reputation as you might expect in a Christian village except none of us really believed them, and it would have come as no surprise if sooner or later one of our crowd got around to marrying Issabell Preddy, but the island had temporarily run out of eligible men by the time Terry Newman met Willie Striker in a Norfolk juke joint and brought him back with him for Old Christmas in Salvo. Old Christmas all the long-time families come together to feast by day, to game and make music and catch up with the facts of the year; by night we loudly take issue with one another and drink like only folks in a dry county can, and of course we fistfight—brother and cousin and father and godfather and grandfather and in-law; the whole bunch—and kid about it for three hundred sixty-five days until we can do it again. A few years back a lady from a city magazine came to write about our Old Christmas, called it culture, and I told her call it what the hell you want but it's still just a bust-loose party, gal, and when the night fell and the fur started to fly she jumped up on a table above the ruckus, took flashbulb pictures, and asked me afterward why Hatterasmen liked to brawl. I told her there's nothing to explain, we all think we're twelve years old, and if it was real fighting somebody'd be dead. Anyway, Terry Newman showed up that January with his twenty-four-hour buddy, Willie Striker, and it was the year that Terry's brother Bull Newman decided Terry was good-for-nothing and needed to be taught a lesson. One minute Bull had his arm across Terry's shoulder laughing, and the next he had knocked him down and out cold, continued through the room rapping heads of all he perceived to have exercised bad influence on his younger brother, including the skull of his own daddy, until he arrived at Willie, nursing a bottle of beer off by himself at a table in the corner. Bull was a huge man but dim; Willie Striker was no young buck but was given to juvenile movements the eye couldn't properly follow— twitches and shoulder jerks and sudden frightening turns—so even as he sat there holding his beer he seemed capable of attack. Bull towered over him with an unsure expression, a dog-like concern, trying to determine who this person was and if he was someone he held an identifiable grudge against or someone he was going to hit on principle alone, and when he swung Willie dodged and lunged, laid Bull's nose flat with his beer bottle without breaking the glass, threw open the window at his back, and scrambled out.

"That'll teach you to go messin' with squirrels," someone said to Bull.

No one saw Willie Striker again until a week later, raking scallops in the Sound with Issabell Preddy. The way I heard it was, Willie got to the road that night about the same time Issabell was headed back to Hatteras from her visit with her Aunt Betty, driving a fifty-dollar Ford truck she had bought off Albert James, her Christmas present to herself, and even though Willie was hitching back north, she stopped and he got in anyway and went with her south, neither of them, the story goes, exchanging a word until they passed the lighthouse and got to the village, everything shut down dark and locked up, not a soul in sight of course, and Issabell said to him, so the story goes, that he could sleep in the truck if he wanted, or if he was going to be around for the week he could come upstairs and have the couch for thirty cents a night, or if he had plans to stay longer he could give her bed a try. Willie went the whole route: truck, couch, Issabell Preddy's lonely single bed.

In those days scalloping was women's work, so it was hard to raise any sort of positive opinion about Willie. He was a mainlander, and worse, some brand of foreigner; out there wading in the Sound it appeared he had come to work, but not work seriously, not do man's work; he had moved into Issabell's apartment above the firehouse and burdened her social load with scandal; and he had clobbered Bull Newman, which was all right by itself, but he hadn't held his ground to take licks in kind. He had run away.

The following Old Christmas Willie wedded Issabell Preddy in her Aunt Betty's kitchen, though for her sake I'm ashamed to say the ceremony was not well-attended. She wanted kids, I heard, but there was talk among the wives that Willie Striker had been made unfit for planting seed due to unspecified wounds. For a few years there he went from one boat to another, close-mouthed and sore-fingered, every captain and crew's back-up boy, and Issabell scalloped and packed fish and picked crabs until they together had saved enough for a down payment on the *Sea Eagle*. Since that day he had bottom-fished by himself, on the reefs and sunken wrecks, at the edge of the Stream or off the shoals, got himself electric reels a couple of years ago, wouldn't drop a line until the fleet was out of sight, wouldn't share Loran numbers, hoarded whatever fell into his hands so he wouldn't have to borrow when the fish weren't there, growled to himself and was all-around gumptious, a squirrel-hearted stand-alone, forever on guard against invasion of self, and in that sense he ended up where he belonged, maybe, because nobody interfered with Willie Striker, we let him be, and as far as I know no one had the gall to look him straight in his jumpy eyes and call him Squirrelly, though he knew that's what he was called behind his back. Whatever world Willie had fallen from at mid-life, he wound up in the right place with the right woman to bury it. Maybe he had fallen from a great height, and if the plunge made him a loon, it also made him a man of uncommon independence, and so in our minds he was not fully without virtue.

_____

Squirrelly finally connected with J.B., who bottom-fished as well, not possessing the craft or the personal etiquette — that is to say, willingness to baby the drunken or fish-crazed rich—to charter out for sport. Likewise, he was a mainlander, a West Virginian with a fancy for the rough peace of the sea, and for these reasons Willie, I suspect, was not loathe to chance his debt. They switched radio channels to twenty-two in order to gain privacy and I asked Emory to follow them over. Up at their trailer in Trent, Issabell had been listening in too; hers was the first voice we found when we transferred. She questioned Willie about what was wrong; he asked her to pipe down.

"What you need there, _Sea Eagle_?" J.B. squawked. After a moment Willie came back on; hard to tell through the greasy sizzle, but he sounded apologetic.

"_Tarbaby_," he said, "(something ... something) ... require assistance. Can you ... ?"

"What's he say was the trouble?" Emory bellowed. "I couldn't tell, could you?"

"Roger, *Sea Eagle,*" J.B. answered. "Broke down, are you, Captain?" Willie failed to respond, though J.B. assumed he did. "I didn't get that, Willie," he said. "Where the hell are you? Gimme your numbers and I'll come rescue your sorry ass."

"Negative," we heard Willie say. "Report your numbers and I come to you."

So that's how it went, Striker ignoring his Issabell's pleas to divulge the nature of his trouble, J.B. staying at location while the *Sea Eagle* slowly motored through three-foot seas to find him while we sat around the marina, trying to figure out what it meant. Squirrelly had a problem, but it didn't seem to be with his boat; he needed help, but he would come to it rather than have it go to him. J.B. was about twenty miles out southeast of the shoals, tile fishing; likely Willie was farther east, sitting over one of his secret spots, a hundred fathoms at the brink of the continental shelf. We heard no further radio contact except once, more than an hour later, when Striker advised J.B. he had the *Tarbaby* in sight and would come up on his starboard side. Back at the marina the Parcel Service man lugged in eighteen cartons of merchandise and we were fairly occupied. Then past twelve J.B. called into us, jigging the news.

"Diamond Shoals Marina," J.B. crowed, "y'all come in. Dillon," he said to me, "better clean up things around there and get ready for a fuss. Squirrelly caught himself a fat bejesus."

I picked up the transmitter and asked for more information but J.B. declined, claiming he would not be responsible for spoiling the suspense. I slid over to channel twenty-two, waited for Issabell to stop badgering Willie, and asked him what was up.

"*Up?*" he spit into the microphone. "I tell you *up!* Up

SQUIRRELLY'S GROUPER

come victory, by God. Up come justice . . . Going to seventeen," he muttered, and I flipped channels to hear him advertise his fortune to a wider audience. "Ya-ha-ha," we all heard him cackle. "Cover your goddamn eyes, sons of bitches. Hang your heads. Age of Squirrelly has come . . ."

We had never heard him express himself at such provocative length.

~

The island's like one small room of gossip-starved biddys when something like this happens. People commenced telephoning the marina, took no more than five minutes for the noise to travel sixty miles, south to north to Nags Head, then jump Albemarle Sound to Manteo and the mainland. "Don't know a thing more than you," Emory told each and every caller. "Best get down here to see for yourself when he comes in around three." I took a handcart to the stockroom and loaded the coolers with Coca-Cola and beer.

Now, there are three types of beast brought in to the dock. First kind are useless except as a sight to see, tourists gather round and take snapshots, Miss Luelle brings her day-care kids down to pee their pants, old stories of similar beasts caught or seen are told once more, then when the beast gets rank somebody kicks it back into the water and that's that. I'm talking sharks or anything big, boney, red-meated, and weird. Second style of beast is your sport beast: marlins, tuna, wahoo, barracuda, etcetera, but primarily billfish, the stallions of wide-open blue water. This class of beast prompts tourists to sign up for the Stream, but Miss Luelle and her children stay home, as do the rest of the locals unless a record's shattered, because these are regular beasts on the Outer Banks, at least for a few more years until they are gone forever, and after the captain and the angler quit swaggering around thinking they're movie stars, I send Brainless out to cut down that poor dead and stinking hero-fish and tow it into the Sound for the crabs and eels, and that's that too. The third style of beast is kidnapped from the bottom of the world and is worth a ransom, and that's what Striker would have. He wouldn't bring anything in for its freak value, he was the last man on earth to recognize sport—all he did day in day out was labor for a living, like most but not all of us out here—so I figured he hooked himself a windfall beast destined for finer restaurants, he'd weigh it and set it on ice for brief display, then haul it to the fishhouse, exchange beast for cash and steer home to Issabell for supper and his bottle of beer, go to bed and rise before dawn and be down here at his slip getting rigged, then on the water before the sun was up.

First in was J.B. on the *Tarbaby*, which is a Wanchese boat and faster than most; J.B. likes to steam up a wake anyway, put spray in the air. Already the multitudes converged in the parking lot and out on the porch, elbowing in to the store. Vickilee came back across the street with her cousins from the fishhouse to start her second shift; Buddy led a caravan of four-wheelers down the beach from Cape Point. Packers and pickers and shuckers shuffled drag-ass from inside the fishhouse, gas station geniuses sauntered over from the garage. Coast Guard swabs drove up in a van, the girls from Bubba's Barbecue, Barris from Scales and Tales, Geegee from the video rental, Cornbread from the surf shop, Sheriff Spine, Sam and Maggie from over at the deli, the tellers from the bank, Daddy Wiss leading a pack of skeptical elders, and tourists galore drawn by the scent of photo opportunity and fish history. Before three all Hatteras had closed and come down, appetites inflamed, wondering what the devil Willie Striker was bringing in from the ocean floor that was so humongous he had to defy his own personal code and ask for help.

J.B.'s mate tossed a bowline to Brainless; took him in the face as usual because the poor boy can't catch. J.B. stepped ashore in his yellow oilskins and scale-smeared boots, saying, "I can't take credit for anything, but damn if I can't tell my grandkids I was there to lend a hand." Without further elaboration he walked directly up the steps to the store, went to the glass cooler, and purchased one of the bottles of French champagne we stock for high-rollers and unequaled luck. Paid twenty-eight dollars, and he bought a case of ice-colds too for his crew, went back out to the *Tarbaby* with it under his arm, going to clean tile fish.

"Well, come on, J.B.," the crowd begged, making way for him, "tell us what old Squirrelly yanked from the deep." But J.B. knew the game, he knew fishing by now and what it was about when it wasn't about paying rent, and kept his mouth glued shut, grinning up at the throng from the deck, all hillbilly charm, as he flung guts to the pelicans.

Someone shouted, *He just come through the inlet!* The crowd buzzed. Someone else said, *I heard tell it's only a mako shark.* Another shouted, *I heard it was a tiger!* Then, *No sir, a great white's what I hear. Hell it is,* said another boy, *it's a dang big tuttie. Them's illegal,* says his friend, *take your butt right to jail.* One of our more God-fearing citizens maneuvered to take advantage of the gathering. I wasn't going to have that. I stepped back off the porch and switched on the public address system. *Jerry Stubbs,* I announced in the lot, *this ain't Sunday and this property you're on ain't church. I don't want to see nobody speak-*

ing in tongues and rolling on the asphalt out there, I said. *This is a nonreligious, nondenominational event.* You have to take things in hand before they twist out of control, and I run the business on a family standard.

Here he comes now, someone hollered. We all craned our necks to look as the *Sea Eagle* rounded the buoy into harbor waters and a rebel cheer was given. Cars parked in the street, fouling traffic. The rescue squad came with lights flashing for a fainted woman. I went and got my binoculars from under the counter and muscled back out among the porch rats to the rail, focused in as Willie throttled down at the bend in the cut. I could see through the glasses that this old man without kindness or neighborly acts, who neither gave nor received, had the look of newfound leverage to the set of his jaw. You just can't tell what a prize fish is going to do to the insides of a man, the way it will turn on the bulb over his head and shape how he wants himself seen.

I went back inside to help Emory at the register. Issabell Striker was in there, arguing politely with Vickilee, who threw up her hands. Emory shot me a dirty look. Issabell was being very serious—not upset, exactly, just serious. "Mister Aldie," she declared, "you must make everyone go away."

"No problem, Mizz Striker," I said, and grabbed the microphone to the P.A. *Y'all go home now, get,* I said. I shrugged my shoulders and looked at this awkward lonesome woman, her floppy straw hat wrapped with a lime-green scarf to shade her delicate face, swoops of frosty strawberry hair poking out, her skin unpainted and pinkish, that loose eye drifting, and Issabell just not familiar enough with people to be used to making sense. "Didn't work."

Her expression was firm in innocence; she had her mind

set on results but little idea how to influence an outcome. "Issabell," I said to her, "what's wrong, hon?" The thought that she might have to assert herself against the many made her weak, but finally it came out. She had spent the last hours calling television stations. When she came down to the water and saw the traffic tie-up and gobs of people, her worry was that the reporter men and cameramen wouldn't get through, and she wanted them to get through with all her sheltered heart, for Willie's sake, so he could get the recognition he deserved, which he couldn't get any other way on earth, given the nature of Hatteras and the nature of her husband.

Issabell had changed some but not much in all the years she had been paired with Squirrelly in a plain but honest life. She still held herself apart, but not as far. Not because she believed herself better; it never crossed our minds to think so. Her brothers had all turned out bad, and I believe she felt the pull of a family deficiency that would sweep her away were she not on guard.

Her hands had curled up from working at the fishhouse. Striker brought her a set of Jack Russell terriers and she began to breed them for sale, and on weekends during the season she'd have a little roadside flea market out in front of their place, and then of course there was being wife to a waterman, but what I'm saying is she had spare time and she used it for the quiet good of others, baking for the church, attending environmental meetings even though she sat in the back of the school auditorium and never spoke a word, babysitting for kids when someone died. Once I even saw her dance when Buddy's daughter got married, but it wasn't with Willie she danced because Willie went to sea or Willie stayed home, and that was that. I don't think she ever pushed him; she knew how things were. The only difference between the two of them was that she had an ever-strengthening ray of faith that convinced her that someday life would change and she'd fit in right; Willie had faith that the life he'd found in Hatteras was set in concrete. The man was providing, you know, just providing, bending his spine and risking his neck to pay bills the way he knew how, and all he asked in return was for folks to let him be. All right, I say, but if he didn't want excitement he should've reconsidered before he chose the life of a waterman and flirted with the beauty of the unknown, as we have it here.

"Mizz Striker, don't worry," I comforted the woman. Besides, a big fish is about the best advertisement a marina can have. "Any TV people come round here, I'll make it my business they get what they want."

"Every man needs a little attention now and then," she said, but her own opinion made her shy. She lowered her eyes and blushed, tender soul. "Is that not right, Dillon?" she questioned. "If he's done something to make us all proud?"

Out on the bayside window we could watch the *Sea Eagle* angling to dock, come alongside the block and tackle hoist, the mob pressing forward to gape in the stern, children riding high on their daddies' shoulders. Willie stood in the wheelhouse easing her in, his face enclosed by the bill of his cap and sunglasses, and when he shut down the engines I saw his head jerk around, a smile of satisfaction form and vanish. He pinched his nose with his left hand and batted the air with the other, surveying the army of folks, then he looked up toward me and his wife. You could read his lips saying *Phooey*.

"What in tarnation did he catch anyway?" I said, nudging Issabell.

"All he told me was 'a big one,' " she admitted.

One of the porch layabouts had clambered down dockside and back, bursting through the screen door with a report. "I only got close enough to see its tail," he hooted.

"*What in the devil is it?*" Emory said. "I'm tired of waitin' to find out."

"Warsaw grouper," said the porch rat. "Size of an Olds-mobile, I'm told."

"Record buster, is she?"

"Does a whale have tits?" said the rat. " 'Scuse me, Mizz Striker."

You can't buy publicity like that for an outfit or even an entire state, and taking the record on a grouper is enough to make the angler a famous and well-thought-of man. I looked back out the bayside window. Squirrelly was above the congregation on the lid of his fishbox, J.B. next to him. Squirrelly had his arms outstretched like Preacher exhorting his flock. J.B. had whisked off the old man's cap. Willie's tongue was hanging out, lapping at a baptism of foamy champagne.

"Old Squirrel come out of his nest," Emory remarked. I fixed him with a sour look for speaking that way in front of Issabell. "Old Squirrelly's on top of the world."

Issabell's pale eyes glistened. "Squirrelly," she repeated, strangely pleased. "That's what y'all call Willie, isn't it." She took for herself a deep and surprising breath of gratitude. "I just think it's so nice of y'all to give him a pet name like that."

⁓

The crowd multiplied; a state trooper came to try to clear a lane on Highway Twelve. At intervals boats from the charter fleet arrived back from the Gulf Stream, captains and crew saluting Squirrelly from the bridge. Issabell went down to be with her champion. Emory and I and Vickilee had all we could do to handle customers, sold out of camera film in nothing flat, moved thirty-eight cases of beer mostly by the can. I figured it was time I went down and congratulated Willie, verify if he had made himself newsworthy or was just being a stinker. First thing though, I placed a call to Fort Lauderdale and got educated on the state, national, and world records for said variety of beast so at least there'd be one of us on the dock knew what he was talking about.

To avoid the crowd I untied my outboard runabout over at the top of the slips and puttered down the harbor, tied up on the stern of the *Sea Eagle*, and J.B. gave me a hand aboard. For the first time I saw that awesome fish, had to hike over it in fact. Let me just say this: you live on the Outer Banks all your life and you're destined to have your run-ins with leviathans, you're bound to see things and be called on to believe things that others elsewhere wouldn't, wonders that are in a class by themselves, gruesome creatures, underwater shocks and marvels, fearsome life forms, finned shapes vicious as jaguars, quick and pretty as racehorses, sleek as guided missiles and exploding with power, and the more damn sights you see the more you never know what to expect next. Only a dead man would take what's below the surface for granted, and so when I looked upon Squirrelly's grouper I confess my legs lost strength and my eyes bugged, it was as though Preacher had taken grip on my thoughts, and I said to myself, *Monster and miracle greater than me, darkness which may be felt.*

J.B. revered the beast. "Fattest damn unprecedented jumbo specimen of Mongolian sea pig known to man," he said (he could be an eloquent fool). "St. Gompus, king of terrors, immortal till this day." He leaned into me, whispering, fairly snockered by now, which was proper for the occasion. "Dillon," he confided, "don't think I'm queer." He wanted to crawl down the beast's throat and see what it felt like inside, have his picture taken with his tootsies sticking out the maw.

"Stay out of the fish," I warned J.B. "I don't have insurance for that sort of stunt."

A big fish is naturally a source of crude and pagan inspirations. I knew what J.B. had in mind: get my marina photographer to snap his picture being swallowed and make a bundle selling copies, print the image on T-shirts and posters too. He could snuggle in there, no doubt, take his wife and three kids with him, there was room. The fish had a mouth wide as a bicycle tire, with lips as black and hard, and you could look past the rigid shovel of tongue in as far as the puckered folds of the gullet, the red spikey scythes of gills, and shudder at the notion of being suckered through that portal, wolfed down in one screaming piece into the dungeon of its gut. Don't for a minute think it hasn't happened before.

Willie wasn't in sight, I noticed. I asked J.B. where the old man had put himself, it being high time to hang the beast and weigh it, see where we stood on the record, have the photographer take pictures, let tourists view the creature so we could move traffic and give the other fishermen space to go about their daily business, lay the beast on ice while Willie planned what he wanted to do.

"He's up there in the cuddy cabin with Issabell," J.B. said, nodding sideways. "Something's gotten into him, don't ask me what." Vacationers shouted inquiries our way; J.B. squared his shoulders to respond to an imprudent gal in a string bikini. "Well ma'am," he bragged, "this kind of fish is a hippocampus grumpus. People round here call 'em *wads*. This one's a damn big wad, iddn't it." As I walked forward I heard her ask if she could step aboard and touch it, and there was beast worship in her voice.

I opened the door to the wheelhouse; ahead past the step-down there was Willie Striker, his scrawny behind on a five-gallon bucket, the salty bill of his cap tugged down to the radish of his pug nose, hunched elbows on threadbare knees, with a pint of mint schnapps clutched in his hands. If you've seen a man who's been skunked seven days running and towed back to port by his worst enemy, you know how Willie looked when I found him in there. Issabell was scooched on the gallery bench, her hands in front of her on the chart. She was baffled and cheerless, casting glances at Willie but maybe afraid to confront him, at least in front of me, and she played nervously with her hair where it stuck out under her hat, twisting it back and forth with her crooked fingers.

I tried to lighten the atmosphere of domestic strife. "You Strikers're going to have to hold down the celebration," I teased. "People been calling up about you two disturbing the peace."

"He don't want credit, Dillon," Issabell said in guilty exasperation. "A cloud's passed over the man's golden moment in the sun."

Here was a change of heart for which I was not prepared. "Willie," I began, but stopped. You have to allow a man's differences and I was about to tell him he was acting backwards. He cocked his chin to look up at me from under his cap, had his sunglasses off and the skin around his eyes was branded with a raccoon's mask of whiteness, and I'm telling you there was such a blast of ardent if not furious pride in his expression right then, and the chill of so much bitterness trapped in his mouth, it was something new and profound for me, to be in the presence of a fellow so deeply filled with hate for his life, and I saw there was no truth guiding his nature, I saw there was only will.

His face contorted and hardened with pitiless humor; he understood my revelation and mocked my concern, made an ogreish laugh in his throat and nodded like, *All right, my friend, so now you are in the presence of my secret, but since you're dumb as a jar of dirt, what does it matter,* and he passed his bottle of bohunk lightning to me. Say I was confused. Then he mooned over at Issabell and eased off, he took back the pint, rinsed the taste of undeserved years of hardship from his mouth with peppermint, and jerked his thumb aft.

"Where I come from," Willie said, rubbing the silvery stubble on his cheek, "we let them go when they are like that one." His face cracked into a net of shallow lines; he let a smile rise just so far and then refused it. "Too small." (*Smull* is how he said it.) "Not worth so much troubles."

I thought what the hell, let him be what he is, reached over and clapped him on the back, feeling the spareness of his frame underneath my palm. "Step on out of here now, Captain," I said. "Time for that beast to be strung up and made official."

"Willie," coaxed Issabell with a surge of hope, "folks want to shake your hand." He was unmoved by this thought. "It might mean nothing to you," she said, "but it makes a difference to me."

Striker didn't budge except to relight his meerschaum pipe and bite down stubbornly on its stem between packed front teeth. On the insides of his hands were welts and fresh slices where nylon line had cut, scars and streaks of old burns, calluses like globs of old varnish, boil-like infections from slime poison.

"What's the matter, honey?" Issabell persisted. "Tell me, Willie, because it hurts to know you can't look your own happiness in the face. We've both been like that far too long." She tried to smile but only made herself look desperate. "I wish," she said, "I wish . . ." Issabell faltered but then went on. "You know what I wish, Willie, I wish I knew you when you were young."

Issabell jumped up, brushed by me, and out back into the sunshine and the crowd. Willie just said he was staying put for a while, that he had a cramp in his leg and an old man's backache. He had let the fish exhilarate and transform him out alone on the water, and for that one brief moment when J.B. poured the victor's juice on his head, but the pleasure was gone, killed, in my opinion, by distaste for society, such as we were.

"Now she will despise me," Willie said suddenly, and I turned to leave.

⁓

J.B., me, and Brainless rigged the block and tackle and hoisted the beast to the scales. The crowd saw first the mouth rising over the gunnel like upturned jaws on a steam shovel, fixed to sink into sky. People roared when they saw the grisly, bulging eyeball, dead as glass but still gleaming with black wild mysteries. Its gill plates, the size of trash-can lids, were gashed with white scars, its pectoral fins like elephant ears, its back protected by a hedge of wicked spikes, and it smelled to me in my imagination like the inside of a castle in a cold and rainy land. You could hear all the camera shutters clicking, like a bushel of live crabs. When I started fidgeting with the counterweights, the whole place hushed, and out of the corner of my eye I could see Striker come to stand in his wheelhouse window looking on, the lines in his face all turned to the clenched pipe. He was in there percolating with vinegar and stubbornness and desire, you know, and I thought, What is it, you old bastard, is it the fish, or have you decided Issabell is worth the gamble? The grouper balanced. I wiped sweat from my brow and double-checked the numbers. Squirrelly had it all right, broke the state mark by more than two hundred pounds, the world by twenty-six pounds seven ounces. I looked over at him there in the wheelhouse, and brother he knew.

I made the announcement, people covered their ears while the fleet blasted air horns. A group of college boys mistook J.B. for the angler and attempted to raise him to their shoulders. A tape recorder was poked in his face; I saw Issabell push it away. Willie stepped out of the wheelhouse then and came ashore to assume command.

⸻

You might reasonably suspect that it was a matter of honor, that Willie was obliged to make us acknowledge that after twenty-five years on the Outer Banks his dues were paid, and furthermore obliged to let his wife, Issabell, share the blessing of public affections so the poor woman might for once experience the joy of popularity, just as she was quick to jump at the misery of leading a hidden life, so ready to identify with the isolation of the unwanted that night of Old Christmas all those years ago. Willie knew who he was but maybe he didn't know Issabell so well after all, didn't see she was still not at home in her life the way he was, and now she was asking him to take a step forward into the light, then one step over so she could squeeze next to him. You just can't figure bottom dwellers.

Anyway, I swear no man I am familiar with has ever been more vain about achievement, or mishandled the trickier rewards of success, than Willie after he climbed off the *Sea Eagle*. The crowd and the sun and the glamor went straight to his head and resulted in a boom of self-importance until we were all fed up with him. He came without a word to stand beside the fish as if it were a private place. At first he was wary and grave, then annoyingly humble as more and more glory fell his way, then a bit coy I'd say, and then Bull Newman plowed through the crowd, stooped down as if to tackle Willie but instead wrapped his arms around Willie's knees and lifted him up above our heads so that together like that they matched the length of the fish. The applause rallied from dockside to highway.

"I make all you no-goodniks famous today," Willie proclaimed, crooking his wiry arms like a body builder, showing off. Bull lowered him back down.

"Looks like you ran into some luck there, Squirrelly," Bull conceded.

"You will call me Mister Squirrel."

"Purty fish, Mister Squirrel."

"You are jealous."

"Naw," Bull drawled, "I've had my share of the big ones."

"So tell me, how many world records you have."

Bull's nostrils flared. "Records are made to be broken, *Mister* Squirrel," he said, grinding molars.

"Yah, yah." Willie's accent became heavier and clipped as he spoke. "Und so is noses."

Bull's wife pulled him out of there by the back of his pants. Willie strutted on bow legs and posed for picture takers. His old adversaries came forward to offer praise— Ootsie Pickering, Dave Johnson, Milford Lee, all the old alcoholic captains who in years gone by had worked Willie like a slave. They proposed to buy him a beer, come aboard their vessels for a toast of whiskey, come round the house for a game of cards, and Willie had his most fun yet acting like he couldn't quite recall their names, asking if they were from around here or Johnny-come-latelys, and I changed my mind about Willie hating himself so much since it was clear it was us he hated more. Leonard Purse, the owner of the fishhouse, was unable to approach closer than three-deep to Willie; he waved and yessirred until he caught Squirrelly's eye and an impossible negotiation ensued. Both spoke merrily enough but with an icy twinkle in their eyes.

"Purty fish, Willie. How much that monster weigh?"

"Eight dollars," Willie said, a forthright suggestion of an outrageous price per pound.

"Money like that would ruin your white-trash life. Give you a dollar ten as she hangs."

"Nine dollars," Willie said, crazy, elated.

"Dollar fifteen."

"You are a schwine."

"Meat's likely to be veined with gristle on a beast that size."

"I will kill you in your schleep."

"Heh-heh-heh. Must have made you sick to ask J.B. for help."

"Ha-ha! Too bad you are chicken of der wadder, or maybe I could ask you."

Vickilee fought her way out of the store to inform me that the phone had been ringing off the hook. TV people from New Bern and Raleigh, Greenville and Norfolk were scheduled by her one after the other for the morning. Newspaper people had already arrived from up the coast; she and Emory had talked to them and they were waiting for the crowd to loosen up before they tried to push through to us, and one of then had phoned a syndicate, so the news had gone out on the wire, which meant big-city coverage from up north, and of course all the sport magazines said they'd try to send somebody down, and make sure the fish stayed intact. Also, scientists were coming from the marine research center in Wilmington, and professors from Duke hoped they could drive out tomorrow if we would promise to keep the fish in one piece until they got here. The beer trucks were going to make special deliveries in the morning, the snack man too. Charters were filling up for weeks in advance.

So you see Squirrelly and his grouper were instant industry. The event took on a dimension of its own and Willie embraced his role, knew he was at last scot-free to say what he pleased without limit and play the admiral without making us complain. He sponged up energy off the crowd and let it make him boastful and abrupt, a real nautical character, and the folks not from around here loved his arrogance and thought we were all little squirrelly devils. Issabell seemed anxious too, this was not quite how she had envisioned Willie behaving, him telling reporters he was the only man on Hatteras who knew where the big fish were, but she beamed naively and chattered with the other wives and seemed to enjoy herself, even her goofed eye shined with excitement. It was a thrill, maybe her first one of magnitude, and she wasn't going to darken it for herself by being embarrassed.

Willie left the fish suspended until after the sun went down, when I finally got him to agree to put it back on the boat and layer it with ice. Its scales had stiffened and dried, its brown- and brownish-green-marbled colors turned flat and chalky. Both he and Issabell remained on the boat that night, receiving a stream of visitors until well past midnight, whooping it up and having a grand time, playing country music on the radio so loud I could hear it word for word in my apartment above the store. I looked out the window once and saw Willie waltzing his wife under one of the security lightpoles, a dog and some kids standing there watching as they carefully spun in circles. I said to myself, That's the ticket, old Squirrel.

Life in Hatteras is generally calm, but Tuesday was carnival day from start to finish. Willie was up at his customary time before dawn, fiddling around the *Sea Eagle* as if it were his intention to go to work. When the fleet started out the harbor though, he and Issabell promenaded across the road for breakfast at the café, and when he got back I helped him winch the fish into the air and like magic we had ourselves a crowd again, families driving down from Nags Head, families who took the ferry from Ocracoke, Willie signing autographs for children, full of coastal authority and lore for the adults, cocky as hell to any fisherman who wandered over. A camera crew pulled up in a van around ten, the rest arrived soon after. What's it feel like to catch a fish so big? they asked. For a second he was hostile, glaring at the microphone, the camera lens, the interviewer with his necktie loosened in the heat. Then he grinned impishly and said, I won't tell you. You broke the world's record, is that right? Maybe, he allowed indifferently and winked over the TV person's shoulder at me and Issabell. When the next crew set up, he more or less hinted he was God Almighty and predicted his record would never be broken. After two more crews finished with him the sun was high; I made him take the fish down, throw a blanket of ice on it. Every few minutes Emory was on the P.A., informing Squirrelly he had a phone call. Vickilee came out and handed Willie a telegram from the governor, commending him for the "catch of the century." I guess the biggest treat for most of us was when the seaplane landed outside the cut, though nobody around here particularly cared for the fellows crammed in there, Fish and

Game boys over to authenticate the grouper, so we pulled the fish back out of the boat and secured it to the scales. Hour later Willie took it down again to stick in ice, but not ten minutes after that a truck came by with a load of National Park Rangers wanting to have individual pictures taken with Squirrelly and the grouper, so he hung it back up, then a new wave of sightseers came by at midafternoon, another wave when the fleet came in at five, so he just let it dangle there on the arm of the hoist, beginning to sag from the amount of euphoric handling and heat, until it was too dark for cameras and that's when he relented to lower it down and we muscled it back to the boat, he took her down past the slips to the fishhouse, to finally sell the beast to Leonard I thought, but no, he collected a fresh half ton of ice. Willie wanted to play with the grouper for still another day.

That's almost all there is to tell if it wasn't for Squirrelly's unsolved past, the youth that Issabell regretted she had missed. On Wednesday he strung the fish up and dropped it down I'd say about a dozen times, the flow of onlookers and congratulators and hangarounds had decreased, Issabell was as animated as a real-estate agent and as girlish as we'd ever seen, but by midday the glow was off. She had been accidentally bumped into the harbor by a fan, was pulled out muddy and slicked with diesel oil, yet still she had discovered the uninhibiting powers of fame and swore that she had been endowed by the presence of the fish with clearer social vision.

By the time Squirrelly did get his grouper over to the fishhouse and they knifed it open, it was all mush inside, not worth a penny. He shipped the skin, the head, and the fins away to a taxidermist in Florida, and I suppose the pieces are all still there, sitting in a box like junk.

Now if you didn't already know, this story winds up

with a punch from so far out in left field there's just no way you could see it coming, but I can't apologize for that, no more than I could take responsibility for a hurricane. About a week after everything got back to normal down here, and Squirrelly seemed content with memories and retreated back to his habits of seclusion, Brainless came crashing through the screen door, arms and legs flapping, his tongue too twisted with what he was dying to say for us to make any sense of his message.

Emory looked up from his books. I was on the phone to a man wanting a half-day charter to the Stream, arguing with him that there was no such thing as a half-day charter that went out that far. "When's that boy gonna grow up," Emory clucked. He told Brainless to slow down and concentrate on speaking right.

"They'se takin' Squirrelly away," Brainless said. He pointed back out the door.

I told the fellow on the line I might call him back if I had something and hung up, went around the counter and outside on the porch, Emory too, everybody came in fact, Vickilee and Buddy and Junior and Albert and two customers in the store. It was a foggy, drizzly morning, the security lamps casting soupy yellow columns of light down to the dock; most of the boats hadn't left yet but their engines were warming up. I don't think the sun had come up yet but you couldn't be sure. The boy was right, a group of men in mackintoshes were putting handcuffs on Squirrelly and taking him off the *Sea Eagle*. The other captains and crews stood around in the mist, watching it happen. The men had on street shoes and looked official, you know, as you'd expect, and they led Willie to a dark sedan with government license plates. One of them opened the rear door for Willie, who kept his head bowed, and sort of helped him, pushed him, into the car. None of us tried to stop it, not one of us spoke up and said, Hey, what's going on? He was still an outsider to us and his life was none of our business. None of us said or even thought of saying, Willie, good-bye. We all just thought: There goes Willie, not in high style. The sedan pulled out of the lot and turned north.

"He's a goddamn natsy!" squealed Brainless, shaking us out of our spell.

"I told you not to cuss around here," Emory said. That was all anybody said.

Squirrelly's true name, the papers told us, was Wilhelm Strechenberger, and they took him back somewhere to Europe or Russia, I believe it was, to stand trial for things he supposedly did during the war. The TV said Squirrelly had been a young guard for the Germans in one of their camps. He had been "long sought" by "authorities," who thought he was living in Ohio. One of his victims who survived said something like Squirrelly was the cruelest individual he had ever met in his entire life.

Boy, oh boy—that's all we could say. Did we believe it? Hell no. Then, little by little, yes, though it seemed far beyond our abilities to know and to understand.

Issabell says it's a case of mistaken identity, although she won't mention Willie when she comes out in public, and if you ask me I'd say she blames us for her loss of him, as if what he had been all those years ago as well as what he became when he caught the fish—as if that behavior were somehow our fault.

Mitty Terbill was convinced it was Willie who grabbed her Prince Ed for some unspeakable purpose. She's entitled to her opinion, of course, but she shouldn't have expressed it in front of Issabell, who forfeited her reputation as the last and only docile Preddy by stamping the widow Terbill on her foot and breaking one of the old lady's toes. She filed assault charges against Issabell, saying Issabell and Willie were two of a kind. Like Mitty, you might think that Willie Striker being a war criminal explains a lot, you might even think it explains everything, but I have to tell you I don't.

Now that we know the story, or at least think we do, of Willie's past, we still differ about why Willie came off the boat that day to expose himself, to be electronically reproduced all over the land—was it for Issabell or the fish?—and I say I don't know if Willie actually liked fishing, I expect he didn't unless he craved punishing work, and I don't know what he felt about Issabell besides safe, but I do know this: Like many people around here, Willie liked being envied. The Willie we knew was a lot like us, that's why he lasted here when others from the outside didn't, and that's what we saw for ourselves from the time he conked Bull Newman on the nose to the way he abused what he gained when he brought in that beast from the deep and hung it up for all to admire. He was, in his manner, much like us.

We still talk about the grouper all right, but when we do we automatically disconnect that prize fish from Willie—whether that's right or wrong is not for me to say—and we talk about it hanging in the air off the scale reeking a powerful smell of creation, Day One, so to speak, and it sounds like it appeared among us like ... well, like an immaculate moment in sport. We've been outside things for a long time here on the very edge of the continent, so what I'm saying, maybe, is that we, like Issabell, we're only just discovering what it's like to be part of the world.

HiDALGOS

You're in for it, *gringo,* if you've been seated alongside a Latin businessman on a flight south out of Miami, assigned to the simmering paramilitary looks that emanate from behind his sunglasses. And the rhetoric will be compounded, you can be sure, if there's whiskey, the ostentatious use of money, and it will escalate to the unchallengeable if the businessman is also an exile or expatriate, making his residence in Dade County, with warehouses down on the river. And if he is wearing narrow shoes shined with absolute principles, and dressed in the blue suit of his moral insight, you should know, *gringo,* that you are in for it.

"What's wrong with Americans? *Bueno,* I will tell you."

He was a Dominican—not only a grower but an exporter of coffee—going on to Puerto Plata. Thus he began to brief Mitchell Wilson, a businessman of sorts himself, not too long after they had lifted off. Wilson listened with one ear, showed interest with one eye, smiled insincerely with half his mouth, all the while concentrating on his newsmagazine. "One minute," the Dominican interrupted himself as a flight attendant walked up the aisle. "Sssstt, *be-be,* two Johnny Walker Negro." He looked at Wilson. "Wha' you want, man?" he asked, making a curling smile when Wilson declined. "Hey, come on, *dígame.*" And Wilson permitted the Dominican to stand him a rum.

"So now I tell you. Americans don' like to hunt when it's warm. This I don' like."

The attendant returned with four miniatures, two cups of ice; the businessman insisted he could only pay with a hundred-dollar bill. There was a discussion and he somehow won.

Wilson flipped a page, not admitting outright that he was indeed curious about the peccadilloes of nationality. The page he had turned to was dominated by a color photograph: Iranian speedboats, machine guns mounted in their bows, the boatmen in T-shirts and camouflage pants and *mujahadeen* scarves. Although most of the guns were bare, and some tarped in olive canvas, one had been draped with a Persian blanket, its patterns aqua, powder blue, swirls of white, and the weapon and the struts of its mount were transformed into a beautiful shape, like a blue heron flared to land on a tidal marsh. Something lovely to take to war.

"What's right with Americans? I will tell you."

No participation was necessary; the Dominican would talk without it. He wiped the long, full line of his lips with a paper napkin. "*Bueno,* it is *fantasía.* It is *el sueño,* the dream, dreamland, *tierra de hadas,* make-believe from sea to sea. Every little insect a *hidalgo,* son of something. No one else has this particular advantage. Do you agree?"

A Korean student pitched a Molotov cocktail into the air. The photo was unrealistically cropped, forcing the protester to act in isolation, deprived of support, robbed of an enemy. Triumphant only in the random infinity of re-production.

The landing gear shuddered into position; the jet banked for its approach to the Salt Islands, where Wilson would disembark. The Dominican neither stopped smoking nor fastened his seat belt. Wilson turned to a photo essay of Presidential candidates, eating the first watermelon of the political season. The photographs had no impact on his imagination; he thought of them as foreign, culturally obscure, void of cause or consequence or even symbol.

"You getting off at this crazy worthless place?" the Dominican said, his eyebrows lowered in disbelief as Wil-son lifted his briefcase. "Jesus! No, you must come to the Republic with me." Wilson squeezed around him into the aisle. "Where you from anyway, *hermano?* Washington? Yu, no shit. *Vaya con Dios.* I love you green-ass *mari-cones.* Truly, I do." And, incredibly, he choked with manly emotion and two tears appeared, as unexpected as guer-rillas, from under the black lenses of his sunglasses. He reached for Wilson's hand to cement their short encounter with a vigorous shake. "I love you fuckers. *Hidalgo,* true? An excellent word. We are all together, no? *Los Hidalgos Unidos de las Americas.* Good-bye, bye-bye, good-bye."

Hidalgo, you'll find no uglier islands in all the tropic lati-tudes than the Salts. Think, if you will, of the drive between San Antonio and Laredo, that dry and ominous country-side, armored with spikes and thorns and stingers. The Salts are pieces of the same geographical mood, chipped off the continent to float in a sparkling paradisiacal sea, its reefs the same tinted color of the glass that contained the Korean student's defiance. On the resort island of Flamingo, where Wilson had deplaned, there were a few hundred yards of expertly paved road leading from the airport along a stagnant lagoon, defunct salt pans hosting junked cars; then seven miles of badly paved road; then an unpaved road to leeward; and finally two ruts across a chalky surface laked with milky water. No dirt to speak of, and no trees: Flamingo was brittle thorn acacia, wild cotton and dwarf palms, pigeon pea bushes and palmetto, impenetrable thickets of cacti and bayonet plants, and throughout the vistas of unfriendly stunted growth, dead, blackened, limestone coral knolls lay scattered like slag deposited from creation's furnace. Yes, ugly, flat, yet where the ironrock of the shore relented, Flamingo had beaches as exquisite as the lace collar at the throat of a deformed princess, and the bone-white strands attracted *turtles*—the native metaphor for tourists—by the tens of thousands since the new runway was built a few years back.

Wilson's government driver veered away from the nearby sea, off the main unpaved road to a lesser one probing lower land, moist air laden not with oceanic brine but with the earthy aroma of mineral wealth, and now they braked in front of the lone few acres of honest fecundity on the entire length of the atoll, an outpost of organic prosperity.

"You don't have to wait around." Wilson removed his garment bag and briefcase from the bed of the pick-up. "Someone here will give me a ride back to town."

The knee-high hedge of oleander was now head-high; behind it they had actually gotten a lawn to grow, Faye and Alberts had, a yard to be mown, probably the first in Flamingo, not like the sand-spurred mangy patches of runners scrupulously tended by the hotels, fed a daily drool of desalinated liquid. The citrus trees were twice their height since Wilson had been here last; pole-trunked papayas and other foliage embowered the tin roof of the cottage Faye and Alberts had built themselves for a pittance. Neems and ficus fanned the lot in back, bougainvillaea with harlot colors, a youthful revolution of casurina pines ... all of this the labor not of redemption—the Salts were in a state that preexisted grace—but of conversion, a gradual and painstaking baptism of pagan land.

The black lab mix charged from beneath the potting shed, barked once for the sake of reputation, and then flopped on his back, exposing his flea-bitten genitals for inspection. The blacks on the island were terrified of black dogs—somewhere in their collective past was a notorious one—and this mutt's name was Blackie, a former runt raised to gnarly island standard by Faye. Tacked to the door of the screened porch was a computer-printed notice, which Wilson read.

SALT ISLANDS NURSERY AND LANDSCAPING LTD.

Hours: 8 A.M.-5 P.M. Mon-Fri . . . except when
• There is no one here between 8 A.M.-5 P.M.
• The trucks are both broken down on the road.
• We're fishing, diving, or partying.
(Wilson grunted—Alberts hadn't fished or dived in years.)
• Alberts is drinking his lunch in one of the local bars, which means we're only open from 8 A.M.-noon.
• Anyone comes by on the way to the beach, we might have gone with them.
(Faye, yes; Alberts, no. He was sick of the beach.)
. . . The nursery will then be open any time that day when we are not at the beach. 8 A.M.-5 P.M.
• Something unusual happens, then we'll probably be gone, but you can come in and look around provided the attack dogs will let you. If they won't, perhaps you should come back when we're here between 8 A.M.-5 P.M.
   If there's a problem, leave a message with Bozo and we will get back with you.

Bozo, a well-known personality on Flamingo, was a macaw, inherited from a restaurant gone out of business. He was a volatile bird at times, not to be trusted with fingers, given to brooding existential moods and swift infatuations. He had been enamored with Faye, followed her everywhere like a psychedelic duck, repeating, as she had taught him, one rudeness after another.

"Alberts," Wilson hallooed, unsticking the warped frame of the screen door. He set his luggage down on the concrete and stood on the threshold of the living area—office, bedroom, salon for the high and the low—lulled by the homestead serenity that was the atmosphere of every tent, shanty, sailboat, or house inhabited by the two vagabonds, Faye and Alberts, the secured do-it-yourself clutter, the professionally makeshift life, as comfortable as a rag rug.

"Alberts?"

So recognizable, this island peace back in the bush. There, on the worktable, was Faye's typewriter, a white hand towel spread over it to keep out dust. He lifted the covering—well, it didn't have to be, but the carrier was empty. No letters-in-progress, reports to Burton's clinic in Freeport, to Archie Carr or some other authority about sea turtles, the porpoises or blue-shelled lobster, the iguanas unique to the Salts. That was over and now, finally—why had it taken so long?—Wilson was feeling it with guilty relief, the subtle arrangement of her leavetaking expressed in objects on the table: a cheap wristwatch, a brand of unopened cigarettes, a used syringe.

Alberts's voice. "Back here," he called, a voice that never got loud without being murderous.

Wilson took the five steps necessary to cross the depth of the cottage, then went out a second sliding door to a deck to the open-air kitchen. Alberts was on duty at the gas

stove, heating refried beans in an iron skillet. They would
be tasty, knowing Alberts. And, knowing Alberts, the glass
he saluted with contained rum and water, half and half,
medicine for the vanities of freedom. Wilson relaxed—at
least the man was eating as well as drinking, not yet so much
a part of the everyday shifts of alignment that he had gone,
as he deserved, as white men were supposed to anyway in
the tropics, to pieces. Crawl on their hands and knees, let
pathos ride their backs like a monkey. Faye had died—
Alberts had taken her to Miami two months ago to do it.
First, though, he had spent a year with her on the road, a
hopeless vacation at the clinic in the Bahamas, then to
Mexico and Arizona for experimental treatments, a faith
healer in West Palm, another clinic in Greece, what must
have been a sorrow-stricken one day return to Flamingo,
back on the plane the following morning to Miami, a damn
hotel room off the interstate near the hospital, from where
she had called Wilson but hung up before she finished a
sentence. Alberts had taken her ashes out to the reef about
a week ago. What was left was to continue the process, a
sort of scorched-earth policy, leave nothing behind, carry
what you could afford to with you in your heart, clear
out—and he had asked Wilson to help if he could.

"Until this minute . . ." Wilson began, his throat hard-
ening around the loss. "Oh boy. I really miss her."

"Listen." Alberts delivered a soothing reproach. "Knock
it off. She's here, she's all around us, you're a fool if you
don't know that, so stop worrying about it." He took the
skillet off the heat and smiled. Even at outrageous moments, even in merciless conflict, Alberts's smiles were
disarming; quick, dangerously true, offerings of affection.
"I'll tell you what her last words were—'Tell Wilson to go
fuck himself.' " He laughed at his own sense of humor.
"You want a drink or not?"

Alberts wore mechanics jeans sagging below negligible hips, belted under the puff of his stomach. The sleeves of his workshirt were rolled up past his elbows, the front left unbuttoned, the tails tied loosely at his waist. He had on a bill cap too, a relic of the Tesoro Corporation, a salvage outfit he nearly got off the ground, and though his neck and forearms were athletically tanned, everywhere else his skin was pallid, much too protected, slack beginning to threaten in the flesh. His beard, carefully groomed to the line of his jaw, and much of his hair had whitened prematurely. He was worn out, had stepped in his mind through the bottoms of his shoes, and he intended to repatriate himself to the States, where he had not lived for twenty-three years. Wilson figured he should stay put, but he wasn't going to say it without an invitation, and knowing Alberts, there wasn't going to be an invitation.

Up until the past year, when she had no choice but to resemble a dying middle-aged woman, Faye had unconsciously, perhaps naively, managed to seem a prototypical hipster, a character in a photograph, taken, say, in 1958, at a café poetry reading. Alberts had met her in the Village, an errant daughter of a First Family of Virginia, doing her dissertation in psychology at NYU. She had known all the writers, all the spooks, the geek intellectuals. He tended bar on MacDougal Street, kept company with the folk musicians, all the queer actors and actresses, but he had been to war in Korea and to jail in Cuba, married and divorced to a model who had been given pearls by Sinatra, as if he, Alberts, a kid from Kansas City, had let his life be defined by Hollywood and the Pentagon. But only for a while; by the time he met Faye he had focused elsewhere, settled right in with the Beats. She and Alberts talked too much, two late-night visionaries; the type of fast and faraway delusions everybody indulged en route to bed. But when they drove together to New Orleans, telling themselves they would buy a boat, neither of them turned out to be bluffing. Alberts, justifiably, had the daylights scared out of him. Faye, goddamn her, was fearless. Some life they were cutting themselves loose into.

Wilson first ran into them in '74 when he was working for International Development in Costa Rica. They were out on the coast, Puerto Limon, preposterous *yanquis*, shark fishing, trot lines baited with offal strung across the rivermouth. Next, there was a copra plantation up north, then a bogus gold mine in Colombia, tedious and cold, unforgiving; a charter business, a restaurant one place, a next place, then still another one, a three-table enterprise; a schooner taken by storm. When her breasts were removed she was given six agonizing months to live. But Faye was a headstrong and difficult woman. Anybody who had ever been in a room with her for five minutes could have guessed her reaction. All she had to say was, *Wrong*. She reserved the right to disregard fatal pronouncements until she was ready to make her own; her revenge against the arrogance of science lasted eight willful years. They arrived in the Salts with nothing—little money and Faye's cancer, two suitcases and a box of tools coated with axle grease. But the archipelago was wide open at the time. The evolution of opportunities was discreet and bizarre. They fried chickens, packing box lunches for smugglers; babysat shopping bags of cash for a thousand dollars an hour; inherited hundreds of five-gallon pots of South Florida dirt, each one centered with a withered sprig, an unlikely bounty from one of the high priests of the substance trade, his scheme to ornament his hideaway estate with flowering extravagance preempted by a hitch in one shipment that led to jail.

Given the history of the first and only nursery on Flamingo, a desolate island on the verge of a boom of speculation, Faye and Alberts were hardly pathfinders forging ahead, come to create the world anew. That was it, *hidalgos*—what had taken place was the alleviation of blind courage, or rather the transition of courage, the maturation of its impulse. Alberts, armed with a shovel, declared himself at home.

~~~~

Wilson accepted the highball glass of rum, adding juice and ice from the refrigerator. Alberts asked what his schedule was. He lumped beans into two mugs and handed one to Wilson.

"Get pissed to the gills with you . . ."

"Ah, yes."

". . . but first, as soon as we can, sit down with the people at the Ministry, get over to Cockburn Cay, meet their man. Does he know how to manage an operation like this? Can he tell a customer from a pH content? Talk to your lawyer, talk to the government lawyers, whoever writes a contract that can be approved. Does anybody have plans to hand out licenses? You have to be protected from that."

From behind a rough lattice screen separating the kitchen from the grounds, its diamonds woven solidly with passion fruit vine, materialized one of the Haitian laborers. His face was a shadow beneath the brim of a straw hat that would have looked right on Huck Finn. He held a fat green pumpkin, an ever-present machete.

"Keep it for yourself, Raicees." Alberts, paternal intimacy in his voice, went over and laid his hand on the small black man's shoulder. "Cook it for yourself and Luciano. Or sell it to one of the ladies in the Bight." The worker held out the pumpkin, as though he expected his employer to take it. He raised his chin, light falling across his round boy's face, deferential and puzzled. "Anything else out there—cucumbers or squash—you and Luciano take it home with you." Faye had scattered vegetable seeds throughout the compound, let them grow wild.

"He doesn't understand you. Does he?"

Alberts shook his head, abstracted, thinking of something else. "Well . . . yeah, mostly. Faye would only speak to them in Spanish, which is better." He took his hand away from Raicees and the Haitian was gone, transported, a refugee spirit absorbed into a manufactured jungle.

"They don't believe me."

The beans were too dry, like spackling; Alberts was losing his touch. Wilson reached for the bottle of red salsa on a shelf. "You're always leaving," he reminded Alberts. "You're always coming back."

"Not this time."

Raicees returned, explaining in his child's English that there was a problem with the water pump. Alberts told him he would look at it tomorrow.

They went inside the cottage and sat down, one at each end of the convertible couch. Alberts and Faye had slept right there for four years, molested by no-see-ums, no privacy, as if they were still on one of the boats, often waking with hangovers to customers on the porch rapping on the glass door—until, after the Club Med landscaping contract, Alberts had added on the bedroom.

Alberts slouched, balancing his drink on his belly. "Look," he began, "the propagation unit over on Cockburn Cay isn't worth seeing. They've rooted some cuttings; Faye gave them a sack of neem seeds, but they couldn't get them sprouted. They have papaya seedlings in Dixie cups. Their shade shed was knocked down in the last hurricane and it's still down." Alberts smiled ruefully. "I'm sorry I asked you to get mixed up in it."

Wilson, now that he understood Alberts was retreating from the emergency deal, was apologetic himself. "I wanted to come down earlier, before Faye died, or at least for the wake," he said. "This was the best I could do."

There was another buyer, Alberts admitted. "A white kid, French, here with his wife and baby. Nice guy, same figure, he's ready to do it, you don't get tangled up as broker, so why not? The government would let this place go to hell, right?"

Righter than right. The point all along had been expediency; swift, irreversible release. It was no skin off Wilson's nose; better, really—an individual with a family would prove a more reliable debtor than any government in power in the Salts. Profits before politics, payments deposited on schedule. According to Alberts, the closing was already set for Thursday morning, so nothing important had changed.

"You can stay here if you like. We fixed up one of the tool sheds into a bungalow. It isn't fancy. It isn't even clean. Cholly still bunks here, or you could have the couch."

Wilson wanted to stay, he said he wouldn't leave until he saw the papers signed—just in case. Bozo came to the door, rocking from foot to foot, eavesdropping, and Alberts flattered the bird, saying how pretty he was, poured him a cup of orange juice, two more rums to celebrate the smooth resolution of Wilson's arrival, the alteration of plans. They might as well go ahead and get soused, Alberts proposed, and not worry about a damn thing. The bird gargled with his juice; the voices of the Haitians could be heard out on the lot, their creole like the singsong of effeminate boys. Boat people, working without papers—

HIDALGOS

Wilson was introduced to something new in his picture of the world the first time he heard the way they responded to their employers; the endearments, the childlike intimacy, a code of filial love claimed by the dispossessed. *Yes, Mommy. Merci, Mommy. Drink of water, Mommy.* I can't believe them either, Faye had said, giggling. Cubans raise hell, Haitians kiss the foot that holds them down in their own filth. She gave them anything they wanted except mechanical things, because she'd once given Raicees a padlock for a shed and he had broken it. Tell me, she had asked Wilson, how do you bung up a lock and key in five minutes? *Poppi?*—Luciano, five years ago, pointing at Alberts's wristwatch—*How much?* Not how much time left to work, because what did that matter, but how many holes would a man have to dig for an American to purchase such an object of distinction? It was only a ten-dollar Timex; Alberts gave both men new ones for Easter, the next available holiday. They made enough to buy their own, no problem, but always sent their money back to Cap Haitien, kept nothing for themselves, like drone bees.

Back on the couch with a fresh drink, Alberts's eyes wandered the room. There was a plaid recliner chair of unguessable origin, its foam stuffing in pieces on the floor, ejected by nesting mice. Nails in the plywood hung with foul-weather oilskins, diving gear, Faye's sextant and binoculars, rusty fishing lures, a bwana sun helmet Faye sometimes wore for fun. A gun rack for a shotgun, a BB rifle for feral cats. A short-wave radio, a citizens band that would have been crackling if the nursery was open for business, a cassette player with speakers wired into the shade shed. The Arum Family—caladium, dieffenbachia, ceriman, Hunter's Robe—was being introduced to Nina Simone and Eric Von Schmidt the last time Wilson was in the Salts. Shells and seed pods, shards of Amerindian pottery, nautical charts, photos of boats and one of Alberts's son by his first wife, now at college in Madison. All the remaining space, the shelves and the floor, were warehoused with books, gorged with encyclopedia, manuals, coffee-ringed alternative-health bulletins, horticulture newsletters, entomology journals, seed and equipment catalogs.

"I have to pack," Alberts said, but they both stayed as they were.

～

In the early evening, Wilson mentioned he was starved, repeated it twice before Alberts agreed they should take the truck—Cholly had the other one—to the harbor for something to eat. The curse of a captain's license—there never was a time when Alberts hadn't taken the most pleasure in travel as a passenger, so Wilson drove, assuming Faye's place. On his previous visit, the final night or possibly the first, the three of them had closed down a waterfront bar. Leaving, Faye stumbled and her eyeglasses fell off; Wilson found them, she put them back on, myopic as a fish, not even realizing the lenses had popped out. A quarter-mile down the road she stopped. I can't see a blasted thing, she said, unable to recall ever drinking herself into a state of blindness. She was more intrigued than disturbed by her condition. You better drive, she told Wilson, and they changed places. A mile farther down the road, a bug flew into Faye's eye; she doubled over, head on her knees, strangled by laughter, whooping and choking that infected the two men until they were doing it too, and Wilson parked in the middle of the dark island lane, unable to hold the wheel.

They had few choices—it was no longer turtle time, the

tourist season. The yacht club, a club more by name than by practice, seemed to be the best place open. They sat at the bar and studied a chalkboard menu. "Get whatever you want," Alberts insisted. "Get a lobster. I'm a day away from twenty-five grand."

"Crown Prince of Flamingo." Wilson cleared his head. "Ten percent down? I thought you were asking more."

"I was, I did." Alberts nodded. "I got it . . . the other share goes into Cholly's pocket."

"What!" In a fool's pocket is where it was going. Wilson had strolled through the grounds after putting sheets on the mattress in the bungalow. Cholly had let the nursery run down. He had lounged out there in his underwear for twelve months, a model castaway, reading mysteries and warrior adventures and drinking gin and quinine while Alberts followed Faye from treatment to treatment.

"Don't talk to me about it," Alberts said. "What do I care? Order anything you want if you're my friend."

Whoever walked in, Alberts bought a drink, as long as they refrained from speaking as if he were a victim of Faye's death. Raconteurs held precedent, anyone with a joke; he had no patience for rituals of mourning. Wilson devoured his fish and chips when they came from the kitchen. The sterile atmosphere of the club receded in alcoholic laughter, and by the time he finished eating, the bar was packed two-deep, the tables occupied in the restaurant section. "Would you sleep with an old soft-brained mullet like me?" he heard Alberts, making the rounds now, tease a young woman out of habit and style, a vestige of appreciation; that afternoon Alberts had hinted at impotency and his general indifference to a cure. Cholly arrived, Flamingo's premier ne'er-do-well, to a fanfare of vulgarity from his competition. A portly London Jew with a tuft of wild hairs on the tip of his nose, no member of

Parliament, no Labor Party wag, was as cavalier as Cholly. Wilson had never known him to wear anything but a uniform of aggressive unemployment: an epauletted bush shirt, baggy khaki shorts, plastic sandals, and a beard that grew high on his cheeks. There was nothing a white man couldn't do in the Salts that Cholly hadn't done—except get rich or move on.

"Caveat emptor," he grumbled to the bartender, demanding his regular tonic from the Salt Island woman. "Let the buyer bloody well beware with a girl like you." The exchange of haughty looks was no more than a game, Cholly's detachment timed to her most poignant sneer, at which he turned to scrutinize Wilson with an arrogant smile. "What brings you poking around?" he challenged, in command of a thousand affectations, measuring Wilson through half-lidded eyes. Suddenly his manner changed and he pumped Wilson's hand, blustering with good-natured fellowship. "Good to see you, sir. We missed having you aboard when we dunked Faye." It was as if Cholly were Noel Coward's younger brother, banished to the tropics, there to corrupt the art of theatrics and dramatize the craft of personal corruption.

"How's Alberts been holding up?"

Cholly blinked, pursed his fleshy lips, acting out the act of evaluation. Finally he spoke. "How the bloody hell does he seem to you?"

"He seems all right. Thrown off a cliff, but the same."

"Ah," said Cholly, "very well then. That's all there is to it then, isn't it. Let the man be, I say. He's drinking himself into the crematory fires. It's a proper tradition here. However"—Cholly held up a blunt finger—"I'm afraid it will not travel well. What shall the poor bastard do in the Great White North? Bag groceries? Carpool with your Mr. Hasenfus?"

Alberts emerged from the muddle and wrapped an arm around Wilson, patting his shoulder. He looked disoriented and swollen, and leaned with most of his weight. "Look who's here." Next to Alberts stood a lank man, square-jawed, a head of bleachy hair, a beard thin and colorless, with pock-marked skin and bright predatorial eyes. He was Scandinavian, a Norwegian, Wilson remembered, but he couldn't think of his name. A builder or another architect—Flamingo was thick with both. "Nils." A fresh round of drinks spontaneously appeared. Nils had housed Faye and Alberts for a couple months when they first showed up on the island.

"What did they do with all the black people around here?" someone—an off-season turtle or escapee from Club Med—questioned the bartender.

"Dey is teefin you room dis very minute," she answered, and punished him with a scowl.

Alberts turned gloomy and wanted to leave. "Let's all go on out to the nursery," he lobbied. "I want Wilson to hear the song we played when we took Faye out to the reef."

"Camilla," Cholly's stentorian voice boomed above the noise, "my dear, fetch us our bill." When it came, a four-page tab, the recurring but temporal issue of honor was raised by Alberts, and so they argued with unnecessary sincerity for the privilege to pay. Cholly hovered over the green chits, calmly unfolded his reading glasses. "*Goddamn it,*" he growled, examining the first column of figures. Nils crushed against Wilson, leaving a wetness behind on his ear as he confided that he would take care of Alberts, and asked for the keys.

"Camilla," Cholly demanded, "bring me the calculator."

Wilson blanched. "You mad Jew," he said, but insults never worked on Cholly. "Pay it and let's go."

In due time Camilla obeyed, slamming the machine down in front of them. Cholly punched haphazardly at the buttons while she stood by, erect, ready for battle, shoulders rolling, never in her life dismissed as a stupid island girl, black and stupid. Cholly eventually removed his reading glasses and tucked them away, meeting Camilla's eyes.

"It's not enough," he pronounced wickedly, rearing back as Camilla feigned a slap to his face.

<hr>

All the lights were on, in the compound and in the cottage, but the bulbs were inferior and weak. No radiant aurora announced the nursery in the sky; you wouldn't have known you were anywhere at all until you made it past the front hedges and entered a grotto of foliage strung with shy electricity. Riffs of Thelonious Monk crackled down the rows of botanic platoons, marshaled in fluid shadows that made the glossy leaves of the sea grapes shimmer marvelously, made the roots of the scheffleras burst through their plastic tubs. Down the white path flanked with crotons, Cholly and Wilson bumped and wobbled, a light-headed midnight dance. Inside, Nils and two girls—well, young women—sprawled on the couch, smoking cigarettes, cans of beer in their hands. Cholly, as formal as a circuit magistrate, fit himself into the recliner, ready to pontificate. Wilson looked at Faye's desk and decided he should not sit there. When he went out to the porch for a chair, the screen door nudged and rattled and he opened it for Bozo to come in for the soiree.

"Oh God, look," one of the girls exclaimed. The stylized edges of her hair looked blown back from her scarlet face by an explosion. Where had they come from? thought Wilson. Did they live on Flamingo? Guests of their fathers, brutal wizards of real estate? Off a boat? Sorority field trip? "It's a parrot! Isn't he gorgeous." Bozo scaled the couch, zeroed in on the females, the gender of his preference, using his enormous black beak for leverage to haul himself up. The other girl sprang to her feet and stood by the rear door, no friend to feathered things, watching the bird waddle along the spine of the couch and stop, inspecting her companion.

"That, ladies, is not a parrot," Cholly said, hunched down, his eyes nasty slits.

"What is it then?"

"It's a macaw, macaw, ma-*caw*." He squinted across the room. "Have you ever seen Bozo at Club Med, Wilson? He is a fan of tennis, he flies over to the courts and sits all day atop the fence—ping, pong, ping, pong—keeping his eye on the ball. Early in the morning he attacks joggers. Swoops down on them from behind. They bloody well have it coming too."

"Polly want a cracker," said the girl on the couch, reaching out her hand slowly. The bird cocked its head, appraised the rings on her fingers; the feathers bristled at the back of his neck, a request to be scratched.

"Polly want a cracker," she persisted. Bozo straightened up, realizing she wasn't really going to touch him.

"Polly want a cracker."

Bozo eyed her keenly. "Fuck off!" he shrieked, and Cholly rumbled with demonic chuckling. Faye had taught the bird to be indignant when people annoyed him with the cracker routine.

"He despises crackers," Cholly explained. "Why don't you ask him if he wants oral sex."

From the bedroom at the back of the cottage came

Alberts, loaded down with clothes still on their hangers. "I want you all to have these," he announced; you could see his mind turning, trying to match the top pair of slacks to a body. Nils and Cholly ignored him, but Wilson and the two girls raised their eyebrows at each other, avoided looking at Alberts. He was entirely nonplussed by the lack of response, then his eyes flashed with enthusiasm and he dumped the clothes in the middle of the room. Wilson stared uncomfortably at the pile. "I've got something for you ladies too," Alberts said, winking, and turned on his heels. One of the girls lit a joint.

Wilson thought he would strike up a conversation with Nils. "What is this music?" he asked. "Is this . . . Monk?"

He was astonished when the Norwegian snarled. "You don't know anything about jazz. First, you're an American. Second, you're not old enough."

"You're kidding me." Wilson couldn't get rid of his moronic grin. Cholly passed him the joint as Alberts clumped back into the room, waving something long and pink.

"Gaw!" The girl on the couch looked at her friend, their jaws dropped, and they both tittered. "Are those dildos? Look how big they are!"

"Take them if you want them," Alberts recommended happily. There were four of them, which he sailed across the room one at a time, flipping like throwing knives. "Someone traded them for a plant. They've never been used. Faye didn't go in for that stuff." Alberts shrugged; after a moment he wandered over to the cassette player. The music stopped and began again, something different, poorly recorded and scratchy, an almost familiar maudlin voice singing about a dolphin. Out of the corner of his eye, Wilson watched the girl with the peeled-back hair handling a dildo, place it to her lips and crack up, raise it back and part her mouth. Good Lord, he thought, don't do that. Nils tapped him hard on the knee.

"Listen to this, Wilson," Alberts encouraged from the corner.

Cholly leered at the girl. "Naughty, naughty."

Nils spat his accusation a second time. "You're too young to know shit about jazz." He was, inexplicably, angry, and Wilson was getting there.

"Listen to this, would you? Do you know who wrote this?"

He had no idea why the Scandinavian thought Americans were disenfranchised from their own music, but at least he could argue that Nils was no more than a few years older than him. He felt his attention splinter. "What the hell are you talking about?"

The tape was suddenly ejected, leaving behind a static buzz that paralyzed the room. Wilson ducked just in time to avoid being hit by the cassette Alberts whipped at his head. An opposing wave of fury surged through him; he wasn't a kid anymore, he didn't have to sit there and bite his tongue and take an offense from Alberts he didn't deserve. Still, he gaped at Alberts, utterly stupefied, and couldn't move.

"You rotten son of a bitch," Alberts slurred, his head wagging, flushed and bitter. "I wanted you to hear that song. I put it on for you. Faye loved that song."

Wilson stammered, he fought the trembling in his hands and knees. "Why did you throw it?" he protested. "Why would you do a thing like that?"

Cholly, firm and steady with genuine authority, rose from the recliner. "Okay, old salt," he said with surprising tenderness. He carefully slipped his arm around Alberts and led him, docile, defeated by the impulse of his generosity, back through the cottage. "Let's put you to bed."

"I'm freaked," the girl who had been apprehensive about the bird complained. "I miss Faye."

Wilson told her to shut up about Faye.

~~~~

Sometime soon after dawn, with the nursery flooding with damp, heavy light, Wilson awoke on his pallet in the primitive bungalow and rolled on his side to gaze out the ceiling-to-floor screening. Mosquitoes whined throughout the room, and there were remarkable conversations, like convergent streams of consciousness, taking place out in the compound. He listened intently but couldn't determine the sense of what people were saying. Jesus—Wilson sat up—no wonder Alberts's going crazy. He slipped on a pair of running shorts and went outside. A woman talked on a telephone, which was not possible—no service.

"Hello . . . Sal?"

" . . . "

"The things people do these days."

" . . . "

"I'll be sure to tell him. Ha ha ha ha ha."

Wilson peeked around a corner barrier, a wall of incestuous vegetation, saw no customers, only a potting table, the aviary of two parrots housed in separate cages, a Green and an African Grey. The Green became a little girl, chanted a nursery rhyme, switched to a soundtrack for exorcism. When Wilson approached, the bird fell silent; the African Grey, apparently psychotic, cowered at the bottom of its cage, its breast visibly pounding, riven with fear. The Green started again, playing the role of an old hooker, and Wilson watched amazed as it calmly mimicked a woman's orgasm, *Don't stop, don't stop baby, don't stop.*

Alberts was up and dressed, making coffee in the kitchen. He moved around with a wooden gait, as if his hips were damaged, and his face looked doughy, his eyes bloodshot. Nothing was wrong with his mood though—he gave a frail smile but a hearty greeting, reconciliation a form of auto-response for both men, all the mornings down through the years, forgiving each other the trespasses and crossed signals of the previous evening. Wilson went straight to the refrigerator for juice and cut himself a slice of papaya.

"Whose disgraceful birds are those out back?"

"Cholly's," Alberts replied. "Cholly," he called into the cottage, "you've got to get the birds and everything else that's yours out of here today." The Frenchman Bruno, the new owner, wanted to scrub down the house inside and out and have its bare walls whitewashed. The Frenchman couldn't stand Cholly anyway, and had asked Alberts to make sure to put him out. Cholly, his nose in a book, waved acknowledgment from the couch.

"The Grey is mentally disturbed."

"Victim of a broken home," Cholly sniffed, hobbling outside to make himself a cup of tea.

Descending into lethargy, Wilson went back to the bungalow, spent a half hour under the cold shower until he woke up to a more tenacious spirit. He reappeared at the cottage in a bathing suit, a towel slung around his neck. Alberts, in the recliner, pawed through a carton of loose photographs, his brief abstinence broken by a rum and water next to him on the floor. Wilson could see he wasn't feeling well either.

"Something to eat?"

"Naw," Wilson said. "I'm going to walk down to the beach."

Who would have believed it, but Alberts told Wilson to

wait, he would go with him. He handed Wilson a set of snapshots while he went to change. They were pictures of Faye's burial, all the local expat crowd and a few somber island faces, going to sea on one of the dive boats bedecked with flowers. Alberts, grim immobility, on the stern, while a heavyset man with a walrus mustache and a military beret shook out Faye's remains from a shiny can, a plume of white fragments entering the frothy wake of the engines. The other passengers each held a hibiscus blossom to throw, or a bottle of beer, or both. Wilson shuffled through the pictures. Alberts on the boat alone, white hair wisping from under a black Navy bill cap, wearing an ironed white shirt and camouflage pants, a posy of vermillion impatiens clutched in both hands, his eyes black crescents behind the glare off his glasses. Next picture, Faye in better times. Bozo atop her sun helmet, Blackie at her feet on a leash, his punishment for chasing cars. Her smile of tenability, as always, said, Your information is reliable—of course, we survive. The young nursery proliferated in the background. Wilson shuffled again and Faye rose dying, propped with pillows in a motel bed, her blond hair stuck with poisonous sweat to her gaunt face, hands together but you can bet not in prayer, and her expression, the warm confidence of belief, was the same, infuriatingly the same. Alberts lay beside her, clearly repressing his rage at whoever pointed the camera.

He returned to the front room in a faded bathing suit and long-sleeved shirt, his legs as pale as an Edwardian banker's. "Can I have this photograph, Alberts?"

Disgusted, Alberts stifled an expression identical to what his face revealed in the picture. "Why do you want a picture of her when she was sick? What's wrong with you?"

His remonstration embarrassed Wilson deeply, and he

couldn't think of what to say. "I don't know," he mumbled. He tried to palliate his request, to make it seem less morbid. "She was the bravest person I ever knew." Alberts relented. "Keep it if you want, then," he said, "but take one of the other pictures too. I don't want you to have just that one."

At the beach, they lay in the shallow water, groaning with relief. They sipped from cans of warm beer and Alberts, trying to keep his cigarette from getting wet, seemed to constantly pantomime a man asking for quiet. "I love this," he said. "This is the life, and I've led it." Wilson pointed out to him that Faye, who had strived for six years to bring him back to the glorious water, or get him on one of the cays for a picnic, would kick his backside if she were there. "I was tired of it all," explained Alberts. "Hey, I'd had enough." And wasn't it Faye who said the opposite of a good life is not by nature a bad life? The opposite of a profound truth may very well be another profound truth? "This is the greatest thing on the planet, this water," Alberts crowed with pleasure, and under he went, glasses, cigarette, beer, and all. Yet by the time they toweled themselves dry and left, Alberts's face resembled a pomegranate, his shoulders and back forewarned blistering, his legs looked like they had been scraped with a wire brush, and he avowed that the sun was killing him.

The Frenchman waited at the cottage, overwhelming them with his energy, his boiling competence. "Alberts," he lectured, both amused and impatient, "what are you doing? You never go to the beach and now you go to the beach? You're supposed to be moving out, eh?" He gestured at a five-gallon drum of paint he had lugged in. "Look, I stole that from the airport—they're too disorganized to know what's going on," he confessed with laughter. "I think it should be enough, yes?" He paced around the room, surveying for other reasons to be there. "Alberts, where are the Haitians? I want them to start throwing out all the junk in the main shed. Today—okay with you? Are they around? How did you get so much junk out there? It all has to go." He walked out back, shouting for Raicees.

"Jesus Christ," said Wilson. "A capitalist."

"He's all right. It'll be good for the place. He'll unwind."

"He's going to burn up trying to make this into a white man's business."

Bruno hurried back into the room. "Alberts," he rattled on, "I meant to ask you, where's the other truck? I tell Cholly he can't drive the truck anymore, eh? Come with me to find him and drive it back."

"Not me." Alberts was letting Bruno aggravate him; he was also in pain, smearing a film of aloe across his skin. "I feel lousy. I'm going to have a drink and go back to bed. The truck isn't yours until tomorrow anyway."

Undaunted, Bruno turned to Wilson, and he agreed to go to town with the Frenchman, not so much to hunt down Cholly, but so Alberts could have some peace.

He found Cholly in the bar of the yacht club, lulled by sentimental boasting, the brisk trade of youthful exploits of his brethren of the Indies Nouveau. Again and again, Cholly and his cronies toasted the next new world, a place where they wouldn't have to give back what they had once conquered. Long after the sun lowered and the harbor blackened, Wilson finally decided that everything—the insanely loud copulatory music, the aggressive glamor of the clientele, the hauteur of the women, the unpredictable rapport between the males, the perfumed crush of bon vivants, the chic Eurotrash, the long-haired renegades with tattooed forearms—*everything* and everyone was insufferable, yet he stayed on, hoping for one thing good and rich to happen, a clear sensation of potentiality without a face or a name to it, and when that too seemed futile, he had one last drink and left.

Driving down the inky island lane to leeward, he tipped his head out the window of the truck, relishing the velvet breeze of the latitude, sighted the road ahead with quick instinctive looks, and mostly concerned himself with the diamond spray of the constellations. Faye, a little screwy, had been a dilettante of the paranormal; she believed in ghosts and the afterlife, and most of all in mystery. Wilson wanted, expected, then even stopped the truck and got out under the celestial loneliness and its shock of stars and ordered her to offer a sign, *right now,* let it be a meteor streaking through the desolation or a fluttering shape, a half-glimpsed animal in the headlights, anything, some message to obliterate the yearning, some gesture that all was satisfactory in the beyond. He waited for a while, hurt by the silence and then cursing her for being too inebriated with death to pay attention, and went on. The crickets were in full orchestration at the nursery; the lights were cut, and the air was pungent with smells of compost. Yet when he neared the cottage he thought he noticed a flickering behind the bedroom curtain, so he walked in instead of veering off to the bungalow, through the bathroom to the other side of the residence, Alberts's sanctuary, to check on him. He was prone on the bed, awake and clothed but barefoot, his skin aflame, his eyes meditating on a lizard eating insects attracted to the candlelight.

"*Compadre,*" Alberts said. He was his most gentle self. "*Tome una Cuba Libre conmigo, si?*"

"*Bueno,*" Wilson agreed, and in a minute was back on the edge of the bed with the drinks. "You making it through the night?" He knew Alberts wasn't sleeping these days without pills.

"She betrayed me, my friend," Alberts said, his voice

no louder than the fluid sound of water outside, pressure-driven from the hand-dug wells, soaking the nursery. "You knew how it was with us. Then she kept getting sicker and sicker . . . and she wanted to live."

Not betrayed. Faye refused to let Alberts inject her with an overdose of morphine, as they had planned, nor would she absolve him from the obligation of his life. He was trapped into surviving her. Not betrayed. Condemned to live by the charity of the dead.

~~~~~

By morning a front had settled upon the Salt Islands, weather the locals called *bleaky*. Listening to the BBC on the radio, Wilson and Alberts shared a pot of coffee. Bozo gnawed on the screen door, wanting social access; Alberts picked him up and put him on his shoulder, but the sunburn was too sensitive, so he let the bird hop around, stealing toast, sticking his black tongue in the pot of jam. Blackie was asleep on the deck, twitching, curled around his empty food dish.

"I don't know what I'm going to do about these animals," Alberts fretted, staring red-eyed at the dog. "I should shoot them, I suppose."

"What shit," protested Wilson. Macho melodrama. "They'll be fine."

Alberts conceded, too exhausted to be offended. "You're right," he groused. The Frenchman Bruno parked outside in a swirl of dust and honked several times before he bounded merrily into the cottage, his personality unaffected by the drop in barometrics, there to make certain they were out of bed, preparing for town.

"What did you do with Cholly?" Bruno questioned Wilson. "Where is he? Did you abandon him last night?"

"Not at all. I gave him willingly to the mob."

"Don't worry," Alberts reasoned. "Cholly will show up. He'll be there," and Bruno, more zealous than skeptical, sped off into a horizon of lowering gray clouds.

When Alberts had brushed his teeth a second time and combed the stiffness in his paper-white hair, they left too. The road was jammed with traffic racing toward them, buses and vans carrying the day shift of workers to Club Med or farther down to leeward, where a marina was under construction. Four times Alberts instructed Wilson to pull over to pick up a walker, pedestrians too poor for transport, old black women toting bundles on their skulls. "Mistah Alberts," the last one said, much like the others, "tank you, sah. Is nobody else does stop dese days. Me hear de news about Miss Faye, rest she soul. We ahll shall meet again in heaven, sah. Drop me here, please."

Wilson let off Alberts at the two-story yellow stucco offices across from the new supermarket, watched him walk up the steps that led to the upper arcade like an old man, which is how he wanted to think of himself now. A person compelled to treat the corners and sharp surfaces of the world with caution. Wilson drove on. Last night he had decided to leave on the afternoon flight, a day early, but at the airport the computer was down, climatic interference, and he wasn't going to get off Flamingo without a fight in the chaos of check-in.

A rain squall had just finished drenching town when he returned to the office lot, leaving behind a lingering drizzle, creamy mud, steam. Wilson climbed the steps, went down along a balcony, opened a door upon a woman typing who told him the number of the conference room. He knocked once and sauntered in. At the head of an oblong table, the commonwealth lawyer, a Canadian, a robustly optimistic man, thumbed through a portfolio of documents. Never had Wilson heard a bad word said against this man. The two of them had been bone-fishing once, in fact, and the solicitor, unmindful of the interruption, rose to offer his hand.

"How's it been going?" Wilson asked. "Anybody cut anybody's throat yet?"

"Speeding along." The lawyer grinned and sat back down. "Keeping these magnates happy." He opened a hardbound ledger of Royal Bank checks.

"You're alive, I see." Wilson nodded at Cholly.

"Quite." Not only was he alive, he seemed shrewdly pleased about it. He reeked eau de cologne, sat composed and erect in his chair, smug with the dubious talent of his resiliency, which could rescue him from every folly but the fractured perseverance of himself. And Bruno, casting thin smiles around the room, consumed by entrepreneurial foreplay approaching climax, double-checked inventory sheets and scanned the contract, his knees clapping methodically, his fingers drumming the arm of his chair.

Alberts—whatever remained of Alberts appeared to have turned radically inward, taken mental leave of the transaction. He hunched forward, his elbows on the table and eyes downcast, sun poisoned, despondent as an inveterate jailbird whose good behavior has mistakenly resulted in parole.

The lawyer tore the check he had written from its book. "Seventeen thousand five hundred and so on." Cholly pressed it to his obscene mouth, folded it into the bottom pocket of his bush shirt. "Cholly, we know each other well," the lawyer stated diplomatically. "When you leave here, go right to the bank, would you please, and deposit it." Impossible to insult Cholly. He was presented the appropriate document for his signature, then the Canadian left the room to make a copy of it on his machine.

Wilson found it unbearable to look across the table at Alberts's wordless inertia, his wounded sobriety, unbearable because his sympathy was limited—Alberts should be stronger, take a lesson from Faye; after all, he was getting what he wanted. Wilson got up for a cup of coffee from the electric pot and stood at the plate-glass window. Behind the offices, he saw, the foundation of another building was under construction. It was going to be big, ambitious, maybe the biggest structure in the Salts, by the looks of it. The first circle of workmen—Haitian laborers; no one else would do what they would—went about their business, exposed to the solemn drizzle, the paste of the disturbed ground. They were stripped to the waist, lean torsos glistening, their heads wrapped in bright bandannas—colors vibrating without sunlight, color full of sap, color that would burst with juice if the surface was penetrated. The men had dug footings that from above composed a checkerboard pattern, each black up to his hips in his respective hole bailing rainwater with buckets and calabash gourds, their dark muscles smeared with gluey sand, ragged pants caked with muck. As Wilson observed their movements, the rain started again and one by one, tic-tac-toe, the field cleared as the men sought shelter. Though he never carried one, he wished he had a camera to record the strangely vital image of the men as the squall passed and they resumed their positions on the checkerboard, and the game started again. He would expect such a picture to explain what he couldn't, to be its own news, about the tides of balance among men.

"Let's wrap this up," the lawyer said as he came back to the table, handing out identical sets of documents for each of the three to sign. "Austin," he called quietly, and waited for Alberts's attention to form before the accounting continued. Over five years of representation, the nursery had not paid a cent to the Canadian. Three thousand—a fair and decent sum—was subtracted from the top figure.

"Now accounts due. Let's clear them out."

Seven thousand four hundred thirty-two etcetera. The sale had been ill-timed.

"I don't like this any more than you do," the lawyer sympathized. "Taxes."

Twenty-five hundred.

"Closing fees."

One thousand.

"Utilities."

Nine hundred something.

The mortgage remaining on the property. Three thousand more.

In the name of Austin Alberts, the lawyer filled out a check for seven thousand two hundred forty dollars and eleven cents, U.S. There would be more, of course, monthly payments on the lien for twenty years to come. Alberts tucked the check into his pocket without looking at it.

Together the five of them strolled to the yacht club for Bloody Marys, but the intended celebration was flat and half-hearted, so they disbanded before their glasses were emptied. Wilson drove Alberts home, put him into his bed, and kissed him on the cheek. After he had collected his gear, he took himself in one of the nursery trucks to the airport, leaving the key in the ignition, and entered the competition for a seat on the plane that would take him to Puerto Plata, then to Miami, finally back to D.C. *Hidalgos* today? *Hidalgos?* . . . Such were his thoughts as he sat alone among the many in the terminal. Nobodys and the sons and daughters of nobodys. *Hijos de nadie.* The saints of the New World lived on in history, but their descendants, bastards of the bastards of the bastards, left in the night for America. Perhaps when they were somebodys, or the children of somebodys, they came home.

Faye and Alberts—their vagabond marriage, the stubborn precious questing of their failures—how had they measured their lives, against what standard? Mitchell Wilson once thought he knew, but now he knew he didn't. What remained was for Alberts to enter, like the millions before him in these times, the draft of cooling current, and without further hesitation or loyalty remit himself to the north.

FOR THE BEST IN PAPERBACKS, LOOK FOR THE

In every corner of the world, on every subject under the sun, Penguin represents quality and variety—the very best in publishing today.

For complete information about books available from Penguin—including Pelicans, Puffins, Peregrines, and Penguin Classics—and how to order them, write to us at the appropriate address below. Please note that for copyright reasons the selection of books varies from country to country.

In the United Kingdom: For a complete list of books available from Penguin in the U.K., please write to *Dept E.P., Penguin Books Ltd, Harmondsworth, Middlesex, UB7 0DA.*

In the United States: For a complete list of books available from Penguin in the U.S., please write to *Dept BA, Penguin*, Box 120, Bergenfield, New Jersey 07621-0120.

In Canada: For a complete list of books available from Penguin in Canada, please write to *Penguin Books Ltd, 2801 John Street, Markham, Ontario L3R 1B4.*

In Australia: For a complete list of books available from Penguin in Australia, please write to the *Marketing Department, Penguin Books Ltd, P.O. Box 257, Ringwood, Victoria 3134.*

In New Zealand: For a complete list of books available from Penguin in New Zealand, please write to the *Marketing Department, Penguin Books (NZ) Ltd, Private Bag, Takapuna, Auckland 9.*

In India: For a complete list of books available from Penguin, please write to *Penguin Overseas Ltd, 706 Eros Apartments, 56 Nehru Place, New Delhi, 110019.*

In Holland: For a complete list of books available from Penguin in Holland, please write to *Penguin Books Nederland B.V., Postbus 195, NL-1380AD Weesp, Netherlands.*

In Germany: For a complete list of books available from Penguin, please write to *Penguin Books Ltd, Friedrichstrasse 10-12, D-6000 Frankfurt Main I, Federal Republic of Germany.*

In Spain: For a complete list of books available from Penguin in Spain, please write to *Longman, Penguin España, Calle San Nicolas 15, E-28013 Madrid, Spain.*

In Japan: For a complete list of books available from Penguin in Japan, please write to *Longman Penguin Japan Co Ltd, Yamaguchi Building, 2-12-9 Kanda Jimbocho, Chiyoda-Ku, Tokyo 101, Japan.*

FOR THE BEST IN CONTEMPORARY AMERICAN FICTION

☐ **THE WOMEN OF BREWSTER PLACE**
A Novel in Seven Stories
Gloria Naylor

Winner of the American Book Award, this is the story of seven survivors of an urban housing project — a blind alley feeding into a dead end. From a variety of backgrounds, they experience, fight against, and sometimes transcend the fate of black women in America today.

192 pages   ISBN: 0-14-006690-X $5.95

☐ **STONES FOR IBARRA**
Harriet Doerr

An American couple comes to the small Mexican village of Ibarra to reopen a copper mine, learning much about life and death from the deeply faithful villagers.   *214 pages*   ISBN: 0-14-007562-3   **$5.95**

☐ **WORLD'S END**
T. Coraghessan Boyle

"Boyle has emerged as one of the most inventive and verbally exuberant writers of his generation," writes *The New York Times*. Here he tells the story of Walter Van Brunt, who collides with early American history while searching for his lost father.   *456 pages*   ISBN: 0-14-009760-0   **$8.95**

☐ **THE WHISPER OF THE RIVER**
Ferrol Sams

The story of Porter Osborn, Jr., who, in 1938, leaves his rural Georgia home to face the world at Willingham University, *The Whisper of the River* is peppered with memorable characters and resonates with the details of place and time. Ferrol Sams's writing is regional fiction at its best.

528 pages   ISBN: 0-14-008387-1 $6.95

☐ **ENGLISH CREEK**
Ivan Doig

Drawing on the same heritage he celebrated in *This House of Sky*, Ivan Doig creates a rich and varied tapestry of northern Montana and of our country in the late 1930s.   *338 pages*   ISBN: 0-14-008442-8   **$6.95**

☐ **THE YEAR OF SILENCE**
Madison Smartt Bell

A penetrating look at the varied reactions to a young woman's suicide exactly one year later, *The Year of Silence* "captures vividly and poignantly the chancy dance of life." (*The New York Times Book Review*)

208 pages   ISBN: 0-14-011533-1 $6.95